A Peak Beneath the Moon

Liza
Home to Hawaii
Why Not Join the Giraffes?
Meanwhile, Back at the Castle
No More Trains to Tottenville
There's a Pizza Back in Cleveland
  (with Mary Anderson)
Peter's Angel: A Story about Monsters
Legend of Lost Earth
Mystery at Fire Island

A Peak
Beneath
the Moon

BY

HOPE CAMPBELL

Four Winds Press   New York

LIBRARY OF CONGRESS CATALOGING IN PUBLICATION DATA

Campbell, Hope
A peak beneath the moon.

SUMMARY: An inquisitive 11-year-old tries to find out
who is responsible for the strange unfinished tower
standing near her house.
    I. Title.
PZ7.C15414Paf   [Fic]   78-20427
ISBN 0-590-07565-9

Published by Four Winds Press
A division of Scholastic Magazines, Inc., New York, N.Y.
Copyright © 1979 by Geraldine Wallis
All rights reserved
Printed in the United States of America
Library of Congress Catalog Card Number: 78-20427
1   2   3   4   5   83   82   81   80   79

For My Husband
with Love

and to our friend
Rennie Brook

A Peak Beneath the Moon

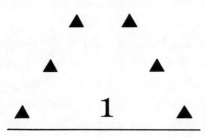

1

THE TOWER THAT SOME "CRAZY MAN" HAD BUILT STOOD IN the middle of an otherwise vacant lot. That's what everyone called him—crazy.

"He must have been crazy to build such a thing."

No one had seen him for years and years and most people thought he was dead, until one day a long black car drew up and stopped at the cracked, weedy sidewalk. A man in a chauffeur's cap sat behind the wheel, staring straight ahead. Maggie's mother, Mrs. Sanderson, and Mrs. McKinley, and the children who were playing outside, all watched.

Nobody got out of the car, but it stayed there a very long time. And through filmy gray curtains that hung across the rear windows, everyone thought—or imagined —that they saw a shadowy head leaning, looking at the tower. After a time the car slowly drove away.

"He's not dead, then! He must have come to look at it," the children said. "Nobody else would have a car like that! With a chauffeur!"

"Crazy!" the Sandersons and the McKinleys said first, and then so did everyone else as the gossip spread through town.

It rippled out from all sides of the weedy lot, spread down the long straight streets and into the center of the business district, to the town hall, and the mayor's office, and all the local stores. It spread in other directions, too, to the fringes of the town, even out to the railroad and the man who sold tickets behind a grilled window. Then, after a flurry of excitement that lasted three days, the gossip stopped and seemed to withdraw back to its beginning.

The beginning was the tower itself that stood so squarely centered in the square lot that at first glance it looked like a counter placed precisely on a chessboard. The children would have played there more often save for one fact—there were no trees. All around, at the Sandersons and McKinleys, whose houses flanked the tower, and across the street where the Wilsons lived, there were beautiful leafy oaks, elms, and maples. But around the tower grew only weeds and tall grass. It was hot there during the summer, and in the winter the wind cut like ice. The weeds weren't even long or tall enough to make good hiding places for children or small animals.

It was as if the tower sent out a message to most living things: leave me to rise. It made one wonder if it wanted to be seen and thought about, the way it thrust up so starkly to the sky. And when people did look up, and eyes reached the top, they were startled—for the tower was unfinished. There was only one side of what looked to have been planned as a tall, four-sided peak.

It was eerie the way that one triangle popped up there. What supported it? Eerier still that at one time it had been painted gold on the inside. Now the gold was just a dirty, faded yellow. Only sometimes, when the sun glanced off the peak, gold sparks glittered, making the children blink and wonder.

Maggie Sanderson loved to wonder about it.

When she was very small she had often tried to make herself even smaller, lying flat on the ground to look at the tower through the weeds, as if through a forest of giant trees. All the other children copied her and then lost interest except for pretending. Jimmy McKinley and Tom Lambert and Serena Wilson said that the tower was a wonderful thing to pretend about.

Only Maggie thought it meant more than that, more than pretend.

Beneath the one triangular peak rose the rest of the tower, about fifty feet high, a rectangle of solid gray stone with sixteen windows, one on each side on four levels. The windows had no glass, they were empty dark holes—the tower's eyes. The rectangular entry had no door; it was open to wind and dust. There were no floors on the four levels with windows. Inside was just a circular iron staircase, winding up and up to a simple wooden platform at the top. And above was nothing but the sky—and the unfinished peak.

"Why?" People wondered.

"It's a blot on the landscape."

"At least he could have finished it!"

"Planted trees—"

"The lot should be sold."

"It's no good—"

"I don't like living next to it," said Mrs. McKinley, and Bessie Sanderson, nodding her head, agreed. "Gives you a creepy feeling, it does."

But the children said, "It's our castle!"

"We don't play in it—"

"But we like to see it."

"It reminds me of dragons," said Jimmy McKinley, who was then ten.

"I think of Rapunzel letting down her golden hair," said Serena who was enamored of her own name, and whose head was filled with princesses. She wanted to become one.

"It's the Tower of Evil," said Tom Lambert, who had just become fascinated with horrifying things. "It's where they lock people up for torture."

"It's *none* of those things!" Maggie Sanderson said. "It's something else."

"What?" they turned to her.

"I don't know," said Maggie. But she wondered about it much more than the rest.

At night she would kneel on her bed, elbows on the windowsill, chin cupped in her hands, and stare at the tower. Sometimes the moon, rising behind the unfinished peak, would seem to grow twice its usual size. If it happened to be a full moon, a geometric design would appear as it cleared the peak—a circle atop a triangle. From a different direction, moonlight would cause the flecks of gold to glint and sparkle, washing the tower with magic. And sometimes the tower would seem to be balancing a crescent moon, or just the point would touch the peak, as if it were standing on tiptoe. Maggie wondered if the moon knew how it looked, being so juggled from the tower on earth.

In bright morning, when Maggie passed the tower on her way to school, it looked shabby and dreary and neglected. Still, she would always stop and pause for a moment, as if acknowledging something, before she went on.

On rainy days it was spectral, haunted, and through slanting sheets of water, looked entirely appropriate in its mystery. Even the sounds were somehow correct: the drive of rain, the hard plop-plop of water pounding down the weeds, the hiss of wet wind. If the wind blew hard enough it made whistling echoes through the open windows. Maggie tried to see signs in the flattened, wet weeds. They would lie in long strands, sometimes pointing to the tower entry, sometimes pointing elsewhere.

But during electrical storms, Maggie would watch from her window and pray. If the sky turned purple the tower took on a bizarre coloration. At the roar of thunder she prayed it wouldn't shake the peak. When lightning flashed across the sky, she prayed it wouldn't strike.

In all of the years it had stood there, the tower had not once been struck by lightning.

People remarked on that and Maggie thought it was like a sign.

Exactly one year after the black limousine came by, the town council held a meeting on "The Tower Problem." Maggie saw the notice in the newspaper a day in advance. It was big news for such a small town and appeared on the front page.

"What are they going to do about it?" she asked her father.

"See about tearing it down, I guess," he replied. "It says taxes haven't been paid."

Maggie felt cold inside. As she had grown, year by year, the tower had become more important to her. She could talk to it, without speaking, of things she couldn't tell anyone else. She felt connected to it in some way. . . .

She went upstairs and knelt on her bed, gazing out the window.

It was nearing summer and getting warm. Crickets sang in the grass outside. The maple near her window brushed and rasped against the shingles on the house. Outside the fence, the weeds in the lot blew gently to and fro in the smallest of breezes, as if the earth were warmly whispering to itself.

Maggie waited to see the full moon rise. After so many years of night watching, she sensed when the world and the moon and the peak would come together. Twilight deepened, and then it was dark. The moon, in the clear, still night, was huge and orange-hued.

It rose behind the tower, bathing it with light, and then—Maggie held her breath—it paused above the peak, balancing there before it swung up and away. Below, the tower was brilliantly outlined with moonlight. And the unfinished peak, transformed with radiance, seemed to shimmer as it pointed to the stars. . . .

Oh, he couldn't have been "crazy" as they said!

But who was he? What did the tower mean? Why had he built it and left it unfinished? And why would he come back to look at it all shrouded in the back of a car? (If that really had been he, a year ago.) Or had he died, and had his ghost come?

Maggie shivered. No, no, there was no ghost, she knew. But there was a secret. Oh! What did the tower mean? It was the only thing in that whole town that was different. If it came down, she would never again see the moon above the unfinished peak quite like this. . . . She would never feel quite the same sense of wonder. . . . The tower reminded her of something. What did it remind her of?

With chin cupped in her hands, Maggie stared out the window for a long time.

And the next afternoon, after school, Maggie went to the newspaper offices.

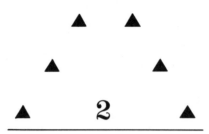

2

MAGGIE DIDN'T OFTEN TRAVEL IN THAT "DOWNTOWN" DI-
rection—only sometimes on Saturdays when there was
special shopping to do. The three long blocks filled with
office buildings and shops were not an area where children went alone, although it was much frequented by
teen-agers.

The newspaper offices took up two huge floors of a
building that also had doctors and dentists and the town's
three lawyers.

The woman at the desk was not much interested in a
little girl who only wanted information, but the reporter
who had written the piece for the paper was. He leaned
over the ledge of the long wooden counter that separated
Maggie from the masses of desks and clacking type-
writers.

He was young, with curly black hair, bright eyes, and
an upturned mouth. Resting his chin in his hands, he
looked at Maggie much as she gazed at the tower each

night. "*You* want to know about the town council meeting?" he asked curiously.

"Yes. You didn't say where it was going to be," said Maggie.

"Yes, I did. In the mayor's office."

"But you didn't say where the mayor's office is," Maggie complained.

"In the town hall!" grinned the reporter. "It's always been in the town hall. Why does a little girl like you want to know about it?"

"I'm not little, I'm eleven," said Maggie, not adding the word almost. Actually she wouldn't be eleven for a few months. "Will the meeting be only about the tower?"

"Oh, it's the tower!" He smiled as if he knew everything about her, when he really didn't know anything at all.

Maggie stared at him for a minute and then said, "Good-bye."

"Wait!" he called as she pushed open the door to the hall. "Wait!"

But Maggie was already running down the steps. If he were a *good* reporter, she thought, he would have put in everything. Everybody didn't know where the mayor's office was. But he was too full of his handsome smile and the way he looked, so he probably never thought about things at all. Maggie didn't want to talk to him a bit longer!

She had to walk a long way to reach the town hall,

for although it was one of the first big structures built in that town, it wasn't centered. The town had grown to one side in a peculiar way, so the town hall was way out at the end of "downtown."

At the main intersection, Maggie looked up at the large, round, old-fashioned clock that stood high on its ornate pedestal. She wondered if her mother would be worried about her, for ordinarily she came straight home from school.

But this was more important.

She didn't suppose that the town council would be very interested in what a child had to say—but someone ought to say something!

As Maggie walked past the glass store fronts of the clothing shop, the druggist, the five and dime, and the odd new foreign "delicatessen," her reflection traveled beside her. It was like a ghost walking at her side, a ghost of slanting glints of light. She often played the game of imagining that reflection to be as real as she was. She would turn her head quickly to see if just once she could catch the figure off guard, if just once that other Maggie would not turn her head at the same time, or run, or skip, or slow down when she did. But always the sturdy legs marched in the same rhythm, the socks fell over her shoes in the same way, the folds of her skirt blew precisely in the same direction.

At the next corner, in the lingerie shop, was a mirror. Whenever she passed this way, Maggie stopped to look at herself with a brief nod. It was like a "Hello! Didn't catch you this time" nod.

She was a sturdy nearly eleven with short, thick brown hair that never curled in the least. Her face was more square than oval, and her hazel eyes sometimes looked brown or yellow or green. They were very widely set apart. Although Maggie liked each eye separately very much, she didn't like them together—so far apart like that.

Other than her eyes, Maggie thought she had a very ordinary appearance, and she didn't think much about it at all. She didn't think about what she wore, or how her hair was cut, and she dreaded ever having to think about it later. Instead, she thought, almost constantly, of other things.

The town hall stood across the street from the park, and had two completed towers on either side. It was a massive building for such a small town. Perhaps, long ago, people had expected the town to grow larger. It took up lots of space, was made of huge granite blocks pressed together, and looked as if it could withstand anything: floods, fire, or even God's wrath. A long flight of steps led to the entrance. The steps were so deep and broad that Maggie needed two steps to go from one to the next.

But they wouldn't let her in to the meeting.

A gray-haired woman sat behind a long marble desk in the vast hall and laughed at Maggie.

"That's in the mayor's office, my dear! It's only for

members of the council. Would you like to tell me what it's about? What you wish?"

Maggie was silent. If she couldn't speak to the people who were deciding the future of the tower, there wasn't much point in telling this woman what she wished.

"If you have a complaint—or a suggestion," the woman looked at Maggie thoughtfully, "I'll see that it reaches the right person."

Should she leave a message, Maggie wondered? She looked around the huge, echoing hall, where paintings of the town's important people, framed in gilt, were hanging on faraway walls. She thought about the "crazy man" and wondered—if he had stayed and finished his tower, would he have become important, too?

Could she leave a message for the mayor saying that she really didn't think he had been so crazy? But they wouldn't pay any attention if it came from a child. . . .

"No, no message, thank you," Maggie answered. The woman looked curiously after her as she left.

She walked out and down the steps, but then stopped to look back up at the town hall. Behind one of those high windows a little group of people was deciding the future of the tower. Did they really have such a right? The tower didn't belong to them. It belonged to him, the "crazy man," and in a way Maggie felt that it belonged to her, too.

It was so disappointing sometimes to be a child, Maggie thought. You could have very deep, true, strong thoughts that you just couldn't express very well. And because of your size, and because you didn't know how to say things, people paid no attention, even though the thoughts were just as real and true as grown-up thoughts.

At least she could *wish*, Maggie decided.

She stayed for a moment, sending out the strongest wishes she could muster toward the windows of the town hall. And then she went home.

Serena Wilson and Tom Lambert and Jimmy Mc-Kinley were all together on the sidewalk in front of the tower. Jimmy and Tom were squatting, playing jacks, and Serena stood aside watching, running her hand through her long yellow hair. She wanted it to reach her waist and kept fingering it constantly, as if that would help it grow. Serena was supposed to be Maggie's best friend, but as she grew older they didn't talk together about things the way they used to. She seemed to have gone off somewhere, way inside herself.

Maggie didn't know if Serena would be interested in the tower problem, or if the boys would be. Walking up, she asked them anyway, "Did you hear? About the tower?"

Serena turned to her, "You're in trouble, Maggie!"

"Yeah, you're really going to get it," Tom said, looking up from his game. "Your mother's been looking for you."

"What about the tower?" Jimmy asked.

"They may tear it down," Maggie said. "It was in the paper. The town council was having a meeting."

The boys stopped playing. Tom caught the jack ball and held it, staring across the weeds at the tower. "Take *that* down?"

Serena stared, too, wide-eyed. "They'd never do that. It's *always* been there!"

"Why would they want to take it down?" Jimmy asked.

"*Maggie Sanderson, where were you!*" It wasn't a question when her mother came running from the house and grabbed Maggie's arm. She panted breathlessly. Her eyes—far apart like Maggie's—were angry.

"I'm sorry," Maggie said. "I didn't know it would take so long."

"*What* take so long! You get in now! And go up to your room and wait until your father hears about this!"

Her mother's slippers made flapping sounds on the sidewalk as she pulled Maggie roughly along. She always did housework in her slippers, and Maggie felt that if her mother would only put on shoes first thing in the morning, she might be happier in general, and less tired. Even now, as her mother yanked her through the gate, up to the porch and in past the screen door—it slammed shut behind them—Maggie thought that shoes would be better than slippers for her mother.

She doesn't get out enough, thought Maggie; she doesn't see the sun enough, although the sun is all around. The house was small, with small windows upstairs and down. White glass curtains were over them, and there were brown drapes over the curtains, so everything was covered over. Even the kitchen windows, which could have caught the light and wind, were hung with flowered curtains straight across them.

Flowers were outside, not inside, Maggie had often told her. Even now she started to say something about it, but her mother whacked her bottom. "Get upstairs!"

Maggie trailed up the uncarpeted wooden steps, feeling the smooth, worn banister under her hand. And a moment later her mother called up, as Maggie had known she would after her immediate anger subsided, "Where were you after school?"

"At the town hall." Maggie looked down the steps.

Her mother frowned up in a bewildered way, "What *for*, girl?"

"I wanted to see what they would do about the tower."

"That's no business of yours."

"I wanted to *know*," said Maggie, not adding that she'd also hoped to say something.

Her mother turned away, not asking another question, wearing the expression she reserved for Maggie's "strange moments," as she called them, and mumbled, "I'll speak to your father."

He didn't understand it, either, but he reprimanded Maggie for going without permission and made her stay in her room and eat dinner there and she wasn't allowed to come downstairs at all that evening.

To Maggie it wasn't much of a punishment at all.

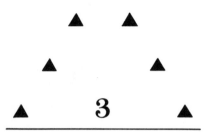

3

ALL AROUND HER ROOM WERE MAGGIE'S PROJECTS, A LOT completed, but a lot left undone. Since she had begun to understand that she liked to leave some things unfinished, she had felt an even deeper link with the tower.

Sometimes Maggie wondered if the tower actually made her leave things unfinished. Now she wondered, gazing out her window, "If I make myself finish everything I've started—will that help keep you there?"

There was nothing awful to Maggie about her incompleted work, although once she'd thought there was. Then she had listened to everyone who said, "You must finish that, Maggie! How can you start a thing and then stop?"

It still came from time to time from her parents, teachers, and friends. In her desk drawer were some unfinished drawings, and some stories begun and told halfway. Her closet shelves held partially woven baskets and artificial flowers with missing petals.

At school they made her take home her unfinished

craftwork, so all of this, and woodwork and clay figures, lived around her room like a pleasant reminder to Maggie —of something.

The things she didn't want to finish right away were always, it seemed, the things she liked best. In her bookcase, although she loved and was greedy for books, were the volumes she'd not read to the end. They were the ones she cherished. She hated it when Serena would get a new book and turn immediately to the end.

"How can you do that, Serena? It's awful! It's a sin!"

"How can you stand not doing it?" Serena would say. "Or at least read the book to the end! Don't you want to know what happens?"

"No! I want to save it, and think about it, and wonder about it!"

But Maggie couldn't describe with words exactly how she felt. She knew that it somehow involved wanting everything to be open-ended. And she knew that she didn't wish to immediately put an end to anything she loved.

When an uncle, whom Maggie had loved very much, died, she had wondered if this wish came from a fear of death. But it didn't seem like that at all. She missed him, and she cried a lot, and long afterward she still missed him. She would remember him at surprising, unexpected moments, and feel sad again. But there was nothing odd about her feelings, no terrible fear of death. She just hated it, in a simple way, like everybody else.

Death was a fact, but so was *life*. And there was the

time after death, also a fact, and the time before life. . . .

Before, before, before!

Nobody ever asked whether that was death, too. Nobody ever spoke about the "before." They were only concerned about life now and maybe life "hereafter"; never about death or life before. . . .

Maggie was just as curious about beginnings as she was hesitant about endings.

Nothing could come from nothing, she thought! There always had to be *something*. Something before and after the middle part where things were now.

When she savored her unfinished projects, the two ideas were always present. She liked to sense the open ends on both sides. This was something Serena had never understood.

When Serena asked, "How can you even *start* a book, then, if you don't want to know what happens?" Maggie would reply, "Because a book always starts in the middle! You never know how or where it really began."

There was no one with whom she could discuss these ideas. She was completely alone with them. But there stood the tower open at the top, unended, and nobody knew how or where it really began. . . .

Did its roots go deep, Maggie wondered, to some long ago and faraway beginning? To some mysterious "before"?

The sky was different tonight. Great gray clouds raced above the peak, covering and then exposing the moon. For a moment the tower would be illuminated, and the gold flecks would shine in the night. Then it would darken, to look like an odd, lonely sentinel, guarding a secret. . . .

What was this mystery she felt about it? The tower was as familiar to her as her home, her parents, her friends. Of course if it were gone, she'd miss it. But that wasn't all, Maggie thought. Why, if it were only a familiar object, did it seem so important?

She did something she'd only done once before when she was seven, and she'd been smaller and lighter then. But the maple branch still nudged, like an old friend, against the wall of the house.

Maggie opened her window wide and climbed out. The branch sagged for a moment, but then supported her to the trunk where she easily climbed down.

At seven, wanting to go up the tower at night, she'd sneaked out in her nightgown, and ripped and stained it. She'd paid for that with something worse than just being sent to her room, and had felt the spanking for days thereafter. Now, in regular clothes, it was simple to climb over the fence. Only insects lived in the lot—beetles and crickets and grasshoppers and smaller things she couldn't see. She brushed them off as they flew to attach themselves on her legs.

At the tower entrance she ran her hands over the rough stone opening. Inside, it smelled of crushed stone, dust, and plaster, and of the pungent weeds that sprouted up between the bricks of the floor.

In the pale light sinking through the windows, she

made her way to the iron staircase. The curve of the railing felt thin and cold under her hand, and she felt the raised treads on the steps under her sneakers. She walked up very slowly.

The tower steps were off limits to the children at night. But they seldom ventured up here anyway, even in the daytime. It was odd how rarely anyone ever climbed up here, Maggie thought. No one had ever complained that it was dangerous.

Little children would dart suddenly, like dragonflies, to the entrance and peek inside, then dash back to the sidewalk. At age five or six or seven they might take one or two journeys up and down again. Teen-agers, if they discovered the tower late, would go up the steps once and come down shrugging. It was nothing to them. Not exciting, not romantic—just a boring view. Most importantly, it was not private. So teen-agers ignored it, and younger children stayed off, looking and pretending.

"But it *is more* than pretend," thought Maggie, slowly circling up the staircase, trying to sense what that "more" could be.

Outside the clouds had covered the moon again, and it was dark inside, between the walls. Some people might think it was "spooky" in here, with just a staircase going up and up in the dark, but Maggie felt a sense of protection behind all her wonder, as if the walls guarded her, mysterious as they were.

What was really above and below, she wondered?

Above the moon and clouds and stars above, and below
the brick floor? "Other stars, on all sides," she thought.
"The whole universe, if you went right through the earth
and came out on the other side. . . ."

She stepped out at the top to the wooden platform
and looked around. It was open on three sides. She saw
the lighted windows of her home across the lot, and the
McKinley's, and Serena's, across the street. She saw the
dull, rounded shapes of treetops in the night. She stood
with the small of her back against the waist-high ledge,
and looked at the unfinished peak that rose before her,
blocking the Lambert's house from view.

A wind was rising and the clouds sailed fast across
the sky. The moon winked on and off, making the gold
flecks on the soaring triangle glitter. Above there was a
sudden break in the sky, a wide, clear opening between
the scudding clouds. She looked up above the peak to
stars so bright and thick they dazzled her eyes. She was
filled with a sense of wonder. Was the peak meant to
point to the stars?

What was the tower's beginning? Why did it make
her wonder so much, and fill her with so many questions?

The wind blew harder and lifted her hair, making her
shiver. She could almost feel the presence of the man who
had built this mystery. Even more, Maggie felt as if the
tower itself were whispering to her, straining to tell her
something.

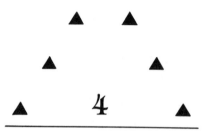

4

A FEW DAYS LATER ANOTHER ANNOUNCEMENT APPEARED IN the paper: Taxes were unpaid, nothing had been heard from the owner, so the lot would be auctioned off, and down would come the tower. Residents would be glad to know the matter now rested in official hands.

"Time!" said everyone, smiling.

"About time!"

Maggie studied the report carefully and couldn't find answers to anything she really wanted to know. She told her mother she'd be late coming home from school one day, and went back to see the newspaper man.

Something had changed in him since the last time she'd been there. From the moment she walked in, he seemed completely interested in her. He smiled seriously and didn't treat her as quite such a child.

"What does it mean?" Maggie asked him. "Taxes and everything. Why aren't they paid, and what taxes? Is the man dead?" (She would not call him "the crazy man" as others did.)

"And why didn't you say *when* they'll take the tower down? And how? And who will do it?"

He blushed, which surprised Maggie, for she had never seen a man blush before. He turned pink around his ears.

"I think I am not a very good reporter," he told her, smiling his handsome smile. But this time he wasn't thinking how he looked. "I should have said all those things."

Now Maggie liked him and she smiled back. She loved to feel any trace of humor because in general her life was so humorless. Her mother and father had little or no sense of humor, and she had never understood her friends who made themselves crazy with wild jokes that meant nothing to Maggie.

This young man saying, "Not a very good reporter," meant he could laugh about himself. And that evoked a humor within Maggie that made sense, and felt entirely natural. Maybe he would be a friend, after all.

"You're interested in the tower?" he asked, really asking, not as if he knew the answer.

"And the man who built it," said Maggie.

"Yes, I should have included all that," he said, and added, excited now himself, "but we must have some old files here. Let's look it all up."

He opened the gate in the wooden partition and ushered Maggie in, leading her around a maze of desks to a door at the far side of the room. Inside, Maggie saw racks and racks of old newspaper files reaching to the ceiling. The place smelled like old newspapers—and old times. There were sliding ladders beside the high racks, and a large flat table and chairs in the center of the room.

"Sit down, young lady," he gestured to a seat. And then he jumped nimbly onto a ladder, went skimming across the room, stopped, climbed up, and began searching high in the old files.

His name was Jerry Forbes, he told Maggie as he glanced at her curiously and with respect, as she waited at the table. Maggie couldn't know it, but she was the first person in this small town who had come to him with real questions, wanting to know more. He was impressed, and it didn't matter one whit that she was only nearly eleven.

He skimmed back with a stack of old, yellowing newspapers and spread them on the table and sat beside her. They started looking through them and, in just a little while, found something: The name of the man who had built the tower was Miguel Sanchez Oliver St. James.

What an odd, mixed-up name! Maggie could hardly believe it, and Jerry Forbes had never heard anything like it before either. They were looking through papers from almost fifty years past, and although the tower had been standing all that time, the architect's name had been forgotten. As he disappeared from the life of the towns-people and time went on, he had become "the crazy man."

Maggie looked up at the young reporter. "I wouldn't

like to go away and come back to find out they called me
'the crazy lady.' "

"Maybe that's exactly what will happen to you!" said
Jerry Forbes.

They looked at each other, smiled and laughed, and
became good friends on the instant.

"How old would Mr. St. James be now?" asked Maggie.

"He would be very, very old. He couldn't have been a
young man when he built the tower. Young men don't
have the money, usually, to do such things."

"Do you suppose he's dead?" Maggie whispered.

"I don't know. Nobody seems to know for sure."

"Why do you think he built it?"

"That's another thing nobody seems to know."

They went slowly through the pile of newspapers,
turning the brittle pages carefully, searching for mention
of Mr. St. James. He had appeared in town from "no-
where" and his history and activities were shrouded in
mystery. He kept rooms at the Hotel Imperial, and bought
the lot which was then far out of town in the "country."
And then he began to build his tower.

Jerry Forbes joked, "The reporters back then were
almost worse than I am now. Didn't give you much to go
on, did they?"

And indeed there was very little.

"Maybe Mr. St. James wouldn't talk to them," said
Maggie.

There was no information on why he had come to this particular small town, or why he was building the tower, or how he intended to use it. And when the building stopped so suddenly, leaving only the unfinished peak and the tower open to the sky, there was not one mention of a reason.

"Mr. Miguel Sanchez Oliver St. James left town today," Jerry read, "for an unknown destination."

Maggie squeezed her eyes shut, trying to imagine it all those years ago. He would have been garbed in black with his hat pulled low over his eyes as he went to the railroad station. A trail of luggage would have followed him: old steamer trunks, portmanteaus, strange bags, and parcels. . . . He would have shielded his face as he stepped up to the railway carriage, not waving good-bye to a soul.

What might he have carried in those bags and parcels? Maggie wondered. Unfinished things, like hers? Books! He would have a book tucked under his arm to read as the train chugged along. But before he came to the last chapter he would put it down and slide it out of sight. And then he would look out, to the hills and valleys rolling beside him. . . .

"Here, one year later," Jerry was saying. "Here's the first new mention of the tower. 'It stands unfinished and local residents wonder when Mr. St. James will return to complete his building.'

"You know, Maggie," he went on, "there've been other cases like this—people who have started to build

things and then stopped. Usually because of broken
hearts, love affairs gone wrong—or the one for whom they
were building suddenly died."

"That isn't it," Maggie whispered, opening her eyes.
"That isn't why he stopped. I know it."

But when she left Jerry Forbes and the newspaper
office, she wondered if she were really a bit "crazy" herself, to have such strong feelings about Mr. St. James and
his tower.

And where had he gone—*where*—when he left town
for that "unknown destination"?

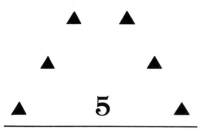

5

"The great Gothic cathedrals in Europe," Maggie's teacher read from a text, "took hundreds of years to build. Under a Master Architect thousands of craftsmen built with painstaking care, stone by stone, such cathedrals as Westminster, Canterbury, Notre Dame. . . ."

At each mention Maggie blinked. A picture of the cathedral and the tower flashed before her eyes. But they weren't alike. They weren't alike at all. . . .

"Now please read on yourselves to page eighty and then stop. We will have a discussion on medieval craftsmen, and then I have a project to consider."

Miss Wiley smiled. She was a round, gray-haired woman whose glasses magnified her eyes. She looked like an owl. Maggie could visualize her perched, like a pleasant, owlish gargoyle, on one of the ramparts of Notre Dame. She'd be all feathery, sitting up there with tiny, clawed feet. Maggie kept staring at Miss Wiley, seeing it, until Miss Wiley said, "Maggie—your book."

She read, and there was a short discussion later, and

then Miss Wiley clapped her hands as prelude to the
project she wanted to "consider." It was really an announcement.

"We shall make a wall-sized map of medieval Europe! Each child shall have a different part to draw and
color—in his or her *own* way," she hastened to add, for
Maggie's school was slowly becoming modern. "You may
draw in objects of interest to you, such as the cathedrals
we've been discussing, or peasants, people—kings, queens
—serfs, farmers—"

Maggie saddened. Miss Wiley spoke as if all this
were so far away, like a legend. But once it had all been
real. Part of the real *before*. Maggie wouldn't like to be
drawn on any future map, as a queen or a serf, or even as
a little girl. . . .

Serena, sitting at the desk behind Maggie's, leaned
forward to whisper. Her breath warmed Maggie's neck. "I
know what you'll draw—"

Tom Lambert, across the aisle, hissed between his
teeth, "Tower!"

Maggie raised her hand.

"Yes, Maggie?"

"Does it have to be a map of medieval Europe?"

"That's what we're studying, Maggie. What would
you suggest?"

"Could it be a long map of the whole world instead?"
She was thinking that, stretched out like that, the ends of
the world wouldn't meet.

"But we're studying Europe, Maggie."

"Well—then can we put stars above it, too, and below? Not just people—sort of the Universe?"

Miss Wiley's eyebrows rose like crescent moons above her glasses. "Why, how ambitious of you, Maggie!"

Giggles rippled all over the schoolroom. Everyone knew that Maggie didn't always finish everything.

Miss Wiley clapped her hands for quiet. "We don't know what the universe really looks like, Maggie."

"That's just why I asked," Maggie mumbled to herself.

She was assigned the lower part of the British Isles and for once believed she could do it, even finish it. For this wasn't meant to be a whole, only a part. But when the map was done, running across an entire side of the room, then it would be a whole, wouldn't it? Medieval Europe— it's time and people caught and imprisoned in a long rectangle.

"You're crazy, Maggie," said Serena later as they were walking home. "Why did you want to put in stars and the universe?"

Maggie lied, "I don't know." But it was really because people lived in time *and* the universe. And maybe both time and the universe went on forever.

Jimmy and Tom no longer walked home with them, although they were all neighbors. The boys were at an age where they didn't want to be seen with girls in public. But they had no hesitation about playing on their own

street, and they all met together on the sidewalk in front
of the tower.

"We have an idea," Jimmy said excitedly. "Let's go
up in it tonight!"

"Yeah, sneak up and have a party before they take it
down," urged Tom.

"We can pretend it's a horror castle—"

"Take sticks to chase the bats away—"

"There are no bats," said Maggie.

"How do you know? You don't know everything."

"Bats don't live there because it's too light and open.
There's nothing for them to hang onto," said Maggie.

She thought they were silly. They loved to think that
bats lived in the tower, although no one had ever seen a
bat. Or seen the "rats and mice and crawly things" they
loved to scare themselves with.

"Come on, I'll prove it to you." She started off across
the lot and Serena, hesitating for just a moment, followed
her. The boys raced each other to the tower entrance and
were at the top before Serena and Maggie climbed up the
steps, Serena whispering, "It *is* spooky in here."

"But no bats," said Maggie firmly. "See? I told you,"
she said to Jimmy and Tom.

They stood looking over the tower walls, down at the
lot and their homes, out across the tree-shaded streets.

Serena suddenly said, "I wonder if he ever meant to
live here," and the boys stared at her, astonished.

"Live here? Never!" said Tom.

"Maybe he meant to build four floors," Serena suggested.

"But not to *live* in," Jimmy scoffed. "Nobody'd want to live here—except maybe some ghost."

"That's what he built it for!" cried Tom. "For himself later on—his own ghost!"

They roared with laughter and Maggie said, "There is no ghost."

But it started them on speculation, which was peculiar. All these years they'd lived under the high, watchful eyes of the tower, and hadn't wondered very much what it was for. It was just there in the lot, part of an accustomed landscape. They'd seen it with infant eyes, childish eyes, growing, going-to-school eyes. A crazy man had built it and that was that. They had used it only for pretend games as the mood was on them, and only Maggie had dreamed and wondered what it might mean.

Now they went wild with ideas.

"It was going to be a museum."

"A watch tower."

"An observatory."

"A castle in the middle of a park. He was going to make a park."

"A fairy-tale playground," said Serena dreamily.

"He was going to lock his wife up, 'cause she was crazy. Crazier than him."

"No, he didn't have a wife. He was going to steal one—"

"Buy one, but he lost all his money."

"He had a fight with someone—"

"And that made him crazy."

"No, the tower made him crazy! Thinking about it."
Tom mused, with a wild gleam in his eyes, "He *was* going
to live here and eat little children at night."

"You're going crazy!" Maggie said angrily. They were
getting silly and stupid again and it made her sick. She
wished she hadn't brought them all up here.

"Anyway, he got chased out of town," Jimmy said,
and ran around the platform as if he were being chased.
"So he had to go somewhere else."

"To China—"

"To Australia—"

"To the moon!"

Having rid themselves of excess imagination, they
fell silent, and then Jimmy said, "Oh, let's go. There's
nothing here."

The boys clattered down the steps and Serena trailed
after them slowly and gracefully, lost in another dream.
Maggie felt like apologizing to the tower or to the "crazy
man" or to both. She wasn't sure.

"Let's do it anyway tonight," said Serena, back at the
sidewalk. She twirled around, running her fingers through
her hair. "I can dress up—let's all dress up."

"Like a Halloween party!" cried Tom.

"It's June," said Serena. "It has to be a spring or
summer festival. We could be knights and princesses."

"No, just let it be haunted and spooky," said Jimmy.

"But I'll have to go through those weeds," Serena suddenly hesitated. "I hate those weeds at night. There're too many bugs."

"Dress up in a long skirt," said Tom. "Then you won't see 'em, even though you might f*eel* 'em—"

"Oh!" Serena jumped and made a terrible face and shivered all over. The boys fell to the ground laughing and rolling from side to side.

Maggie's mother came out from the house and beckoned to her. "I have to go," she said.

"Want to come with us tonight?" Jimmy sat up on his knees and looked at her. His face was red with laughing; he had dirt stains on his cheeks and he looked wild—and sort of horrible, Maggie thought.

"No," she said, wishing they wouldn't go, either. They didn't belong, the way they were acting about it.

"Maggie is a coward! She'll only go up in the daytime!" the boys began chanting.

"Oh, come with us, Maggie," Serena begged. "I don't want to go if you don't."

"I don't want to," said Maggie. She knew perfectly well that Serena would have a wonderful time all by herself, being one princess with two knights.

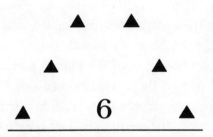

6

SHE HAD TO GO TO THE STORE FOR HER MOTHER, WHO WAS already beginning to suffer in the warm weather. She perspired so easily. Her face grew damp at the slightest heat and stayed flushed all summer. Although it was only early June, she was already in a sleeveless cotton dress and had pinned her hair tight above her neck. She complained about having to use the stove.

"If you got out and walked more, Mother—"

But Bessie Sanderson wouldn't listen. She sat down to rest in the dark parlor while Maggie went on her errand.

She was worried about her mother who didn't seem completely well. And she made things worse for herself than need be, Maggie thought. She wanted a roast for dinner. Why did she use the oven when she felt so hot and tired? Why stand peeling potatoes when she could have done it sitting down? Why didn't she go outside where it was cooler, and take off her slippers and feel the grass under her feet?

But Maggie felt a pang when she thought anything critical. She dearly loved her heavy, generally placid mother who read magazines and kept a neat house and was a friendly neighbor. She loved the feel and the scent of her, which was always of the talcum powder she used. It didn't matter that there was always an air of sadness, or sameness, about her mother. And it didn't matter that she could never ask or answer an important question.

Neither could Maggie's father, who worked in a factory on the other side of town, and had the same air of sameness as he took his shabby car with his lunch pail to work each day, and came home to read the newspaper.

Maggie loved them both fiercely. And sometimes, when she was plagued with her thoughts of beginnings and endings, of the universe, she would run to that love which always protected her. Her feeling, that she and her parents were all of one skin, would bring her to earth where she was small and content.

But sometimes she loved them so much, and through them the rest of the world—as if they were channels— that she felt she couldn't stand it. Oddly, those were the times when she became difficult—"strange"—and un- yielding.

The wide trees overhead shaded Maggie on her way to the store and back. She was again caught in this love for her parents, and it was a soft, comforting, little-girl sensation to be carrying the paper bags, doing something so homey and ordinary. She smelled the raw meat of the roast-to-be and the pungent onions. The pinked top of the bags tickled her chin, and she tried to stay there, away from thoughts of the tower or the universe.

She played an alternating game with the sidewalk squares, hearing the click-click of her leather heels as she zigzagged, one square to the right, one to the left . . . and then walked with one foot directly in front of the other across the white line painted on the street.

Oh, she loved these grave and ordinary moments when she felt herself so deeply inside that she could almost smell her own body—the way a dog scents a friend. At these moments Maggie knew and accepted herself, inside and outside, as a part of everything that was, now and before, and would be forever.

She shifted the paper bags up higher and noticed how the sun, filtering through the leaves, glinted on the fine, thin hair on her arms. Inside each one there might be a whole universe, with other suns, and galaxies. . . .

No! She didn't want to think of these things now.

When she'd first had thoughts like these, several years ago, they had given her a wonderful, peaceful feeling. She seemed to belong to her thoughts, just as they belonged to her. But it was a peace and belonging apart from her life with her parents. The ideas comforted her *up*, and spread her out, very wide, to connect with everything—although after a time it could change to disturbance.

Now she wanted to feel that other deep part that

belonged here, close to the earth and her parents, that included the echo of her heels and the rustling leaves and the warm sun on her arms.

She stood across the street from her house. Her father was just parking the old car in front of the garage. From this angle, the unfinished peak on the tower was fore-shortened. Maggie wondered again—she couldn't help it. The tower always made her wonder. Suppose it were finished? Suppose there were three more triangles, all meeting together, soaring high into a spire. . . . Then it would be ended, wouldn't it—or would it? She tried to visualize it with all the windows in, and with the door, and the completed spire rising from the lot planted with trees and gardens like the "fairy-tale playground" Serena had mentioned. Would it really be finished then? Maybe nothing was ever ended or finished. . . .

Anyway, it wouldn't be the special thing it was now.

Suddenly Maggie ran across the street, pounding her heels hard on the pavement, making them give off a different sound. She kicked open the gate with one foot and then stepped on tiptoe, making no sound at all, up the path to the porch.

"Maggie!"

Her father opened the screen door. "Your mother says she's too tired to cook tonight. We'll all go out to dinner."

They almost never went out to dinner!

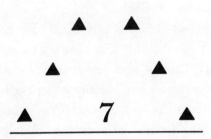

7

I̲T̲ ̲W̲A̲S̲ ̲A̲ ̲R̲A̲R̲E̲ ̲T̲R̲E̲A̲T̲ ̲T̲O̲ ̲S̲I̲T̲ ̲I̲N̲ ̲A̲ ̲R̲E̲S̲T̲A̲U̲R̲A̲N̲T̲ ̲A̲N̲D̲ ̲B̲E̲
served. Maggie's father's round face, with its bright blue
eyes and wide mouth, looked brighter and sharper than
usual. Her mother was dressed for the occasion in a dark
dress and shoes. Although she kept her hair pinned up,
and her face was still flushed, she looked more alive—and
happier—than Maggie could remember seeing her in a
long time.

The last time they had all "eaten out" was two years
ago.

The restaurant was out at the end of town, and it was
new, white, and plain, but there were water glasses on the
white tablecloth and white cloth napkins. The food was
good: plain American fried chicken, pot roast, and veal
cutlets.

At many of the tables, people knew each other and
were talking. They were festive, excited over news about
the tower, and called from table to table.

"Lot's going to be auctioned."

"Why not buy it, Herbie?"

"Too expensive. Sure to be. Things have gone up."

"Lowry's going to buy it and build a store."

"He can't. That lot's not commercially zoned."

Maggie watched her parents gossiping happily—she hadn't seen them like this in years. Was it really the heat and not wishing to use the oven that had brought them out? Or was it the tower, which seemed to be on everyone's mind?

"Why is everybody so glad about the tower coming down?" she asked her mother.

Mrs. Sanderson, her cheeks pink, her eyes smiling, said, "Because something new will be going up."

So. The tower, the one different thing in the whole town, had to be replaced with something newer which would be different for a while, but only a while. And the very thought of "something new" made Maggie's mother seem younger and happier.

Why couldn't anybody see that the tower was still "new"?

Wasn't anything that wasn't understood *always* new?

But Maggie understood something. To her mother and to everyone else, it seemed, the tower had become old and shabby and part of the sameness that circled around all of their lives.

Later, when Maggie was supposed to be planning her part of the wall map for homework, she lay instead on her bed, listening for sounds from outside. Would Jimmy and Tom and Serena really do it? They'd never been interested in "sneaking" up to the tower before. Now that it was coming down, would everybody be interested?

Night had cooled the day's heat, and a wind rushed in, billowing the curtains like sails. Maggie drew up the patchwork quilt from the foot of her bed. She had made it herself with only a little help from her mother, and it wasn't very large; it hardly covered her. She felt the two sides of varied texture and gaudily colored material; there was some cotton stuffing leaking out in between. She held it, trying not to pull at the cotton, as she listened for sounds of Jimmy and Tom and Serena . . . and then fell fast asleep.

A light woke Maggie. Something very bright flashing before her eyes. It took a few moments to realize it was a flickering reflection on her wall. She threw off the quilt and crept down on her bed to look out the window. She saw the top of the tower in flames.

Red and purple licked the sky—long, fiery fingers— as if grass and weeds were rising to visit the tower top in ribbons as gaudy as her patchwork quilt.

She held to the windowsill, knowing that stone didn't burn; it must be the wooden platform burning at the top of the stairs. Watching the flames, her body sagged. She didn't feel the familiar cracked edge of the sill, but seemed to feel instead the searing iron rail of the staircase in the tower.

Up and up, the flames shot into the sky, lighting the grass and weeds, illuminating the gray stones and empty windows that now gleamed red.

Maggie thought of the "crazy" man first, and then remembered the children, and saw them at the edge of the lot when she finally took her eyes away from the tower. They were scampering to and fro like the bats they'd hoped to find, and Serena was a pale, moonlit, fire-lit, ghostly, long-gowned silly creature. . . .

What had they done?

Noises began all around, of voices and slamming doors and calls, and loud yells for missing children.

And when they were found, Maggie could hear in the change of tone, after anger and promises of punishment . . . a jeering attitude toward the tower.

Get the kids inside! Give them a good hiding! Never should have been there! Dangerous to play with fire!

But then. . . . Better than breaking it down! The kids made a start! Save the town money!

Then she watched, as all the neighbors watched, the peak on the top, as the flames shot straight through it. From her head-on view the triangle grew like a peculiar pointed plant, out of a mass of golden, red, violet, orange, and hot purple leaves. . . .

She waited for it to fall. It was the only part of the tower that could have been weakened, that could fall now. . . . She held her breath, her whole body straining, "Don't let it fall. Oh, please don't let it fall. . . ."

Another high-spurting finger of blood-red flame shot up, like the last arrow in a battle. It pierced the peak, shattered, and fled above, sending sparks out in a wide fan.

The tower slowly grew dark again in the night. Brief, scattered lights flashed like fireflies near the top for a while, and then subsided. The moon ducked behind a cloud and then slid sideways, as if peeking out to look.

And between the light moon and the pale clouds and the echo of firelight still hovering around the tower, everyone saw that the lone triangle remained. It was dark now, blacker than the deep, navy-blue sky. But it was still there, that same peak beneath the moon.

Maggie dropped her head on her hands and cried, and later felt sick to her stomach.

All over town the next day, people said it was remarkable.

And the next day Maggie went into the tower and smelled the burned wood. It lay in charred pieces and lumps of ash all over the iron staircase. Drifting particles of ash curled up around her as she walked up the spiraling steps. The iron railing was still warm under her hand. At the top there was no longer a platform to step onto; there was only a gap, dropping to the distance far below.

She gripped the railing and looked up at the peak—charred and black, with not a speck of gold left on it.

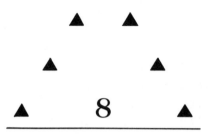

8

Serena and Tom and Jimmy were all severely punished. Everyone knew what had happened. They had tried to make a little fire in a pot to toast cheese sandwiches.

When Serena was allowed to play again, three days later, she was pale and subdued and had her hair in a tight braid. She wasn't stroking it and she seemed more like Maggie's friend again.

"Why did you do it?" Maggie asked, facing her squarely.

"We didn't mean to, and we didn't like it when it happened. It was scary."

"We're sorry," said Tom.

"Why are you sorry?" Maggie wanted to know.

"Because now we can't go up there anymore. The floor is gone."

"But you hardly ever went up before," said Maggie.

"I did, a couple of times," said Jimmy.

"I did, too," said Tom.

"I only went up once by myself," said Serena, her mouth working strangely. "And now I can't, ever again."

They sat on the curb across from the tower, chins in hands, like a frieze of Thinkers, staring at it. Above the weeds, clouds of midges made swirling movements, and larger shapes of bumblebees darted and droned. The air was filled with early summer pollen.

"Since they're going to take it down anyway," Tom said rather wildly, "maybe we should help 'em out."

Jimmy got excited. "If there was glass in those windows we could smash it—"

"Crack it."

"Into smitherens!"

"We could still help—we could throw stones at it."

They giggled nervously and then subsided. Serena just sat staring at the tower. Maggie turned her head to look at all of them. Stone at stone. . . .

"What do you think they'll put there instead?" asked Tom.

"A house," said Jimmy. He picked up a small pebble from the street and threw it.

They tried to visualize a house. Squat, compact, low, and barren at first in the lot, and then maybe shaded with planted trees.

Serena shivered. "I wouldn't like to live in any house they put there."

"Why not?" asked Maggie quickly.

Serena struggled, then shrugged her shoulders. "It—it wouldn't belong."

Maggie's heart began to pound.

"How do you think they'll take it down?" asked Tom.

"They'll break it up," said Jimmy, "with one of those big machines."

"Maybe it's too strong," said Tom. "Maybe they can't do it."

"Oh, they'll do it. That big ball swings from a crane and smashes everything apart. It'll all tumble down."

Their eyes traveled up to the charred black triangle and all thought the same thing.

"But maybe that'll stay up forever," said Jimmy. "Wouldn't you like to see that? Just hanging there forever in the sky."

"Nothing will ever take that down."

Maggie's heart beat faster and faster and finally the words pushed out. "Why do you like the tower?"

Three startled faces looked at her. Jimmy's nose was already sunburned and peeling. Tom's freckles were spreading in great tan pools all over his face. Serena, with her skinned, washed-out look, seemed five years younger.

They had never thought of "liking" the tower before.

"Because—"

"Because—"

"It's different," Serena whispered.

They all felt the familiar town reaching out and encircling them.

"Let's try to keep it!" Maggie said.

"How?" asked the others at once.

"I—I could try to find the man who built it."

"The crazy man? He's dead!" said Tom.

"Maybe he isn't," said Maggie.

"Yes, he is. He came by last year in a big black car and he never came back," said Jimmy. "So he must be dead."

"And my Dad said he didn't pay his taxes, so that proves it," said Tom. "That's why they can take down the tower."

"And sell the lot," said Serena.

"Hey—maybe we could all buy the lot!" Tom yelled and they all burst out laughing.

Serena said, "Maybe it wasn't him in that car. Maybe it was somebody else—somebody who wanted to buy the tower."

"Oh, it was him," said Tom.

"How do you know?"

"Because of the curtains! They were all around the inside of the car. Who'd have curtains like that—unless he was crazy?"

Laughter again, and Maggie began to wonder if they were really serious about the tower after all. Maybe she'd been wrong about them. But then Jimmy turned to her quietly, "We don't even know his name, Maggie."

"I can find out, maybe." She didn't tell them she already knew. She wasn't that sure of them yet.

"But even if he isn't dead, and even if you could find him," said Serena, "what could you ask him? 'Please pay your taxes'?"

She meant it seriously, but the boys laughed again. "Yes, pay your taxes so we can keep the tower!" Tom scratched his nose. "Doesn't make sense, does it?"

"Is that what you'd tell him?" asked Jimmy.

"I—I don't know," said Maggie helplessly.

"And if he isn't dead," said Tom, "why isn't he paying his taxes?"

"Maybe he doesn't have any money," said Jimmy in a practical way.

"Maybe he isn't interested anymore," said Serena.

That gave Maggie a worry because she felt some truth in it. And if he wasn't interested anymore—why not?

She got up from the curb. Her skirt was dusty where she'd been sitting. "Look, if I can find him, may I tell him that we *all* want to keep the tower?" Somehow she felt that might be important.

"Sure, sure," the boys said, and Serena even added, "I hope you do find him, Maggie."

As she walked away Maggie realized that Serena hadn't said one silly word all afternoon. Nor had she once stroked her braid.

Something had changed in all of them since the fire.

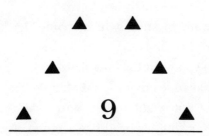

9

THE HOTEL WHERE MR. ST. JAMES HAD STAYED SO LONG AGO was now in the shabbiest part of town. It was squeezed between two storefronts; hardware on one side, farmer's machinery on the other. It was only four stories high and the front was made of yellow shingles, now broken, rickety, and sagging.

Maggie stood outside trying to imagine what it might once have looked like, standing free and upright. Perhaps there had been trees on either side, and it had looked imposing. It was still called the Hotel Imperial. "Mr. St. James has taken rooms at the Hotel Imperial," the old newspaper had said, as if it were an important place.

She went into the lobby.

The flowered carpet was threadbare, and the large, overstuffed furniture was slick and greasy with age. To her left was a desk with a honeycomb of boxes behind, and a sharp-looking man with slicked-down black hair sat there.

He looked upset to see a child in the place, and at first he wouldn't give her any information.

"I just want to know which rooms Mr. . . . the man who built the tower lived in."

"Why do you want to know that?"

"I—I'd like to see them," said Maggie.

"Why do you want to see 'em?" He peered at her suspiciously, cocking his head like a crow, or a bad, black raven, thought Maggie.

She had never thought of lying about it, and didn't know what to say. He'd never understand that she wanted to see the rooms to get closer to Mr. St. James, to see if she could feel something about him—even to sense whether he was alive or dead.

The man lost interest in his own question. "Oh, who cares?" he said, looking back to his magazine. He waved at a flight of steps. "Everyone here knows where the crazy man lived. One flight up in the back, number 27. It's open."

She ran up the steps and down the narrow dark hall to the rear of the building. The last door to her right was number 27. It had an old, round brass doorknob. She turned it and went in. The carpet had the same faded flower pattern as the hall and lobby. Cheap new curtains had been hung at the high windows. The bed might have been the same one he slept in, for it was very old with a high brass head. There was new maple furniture: a bureau, desk, and chairs. The bathroom had an enormous tub on clawed iron feet—and there was another door in the bathroom.

Maggie tried the handle and it opened into another huge, high-ceilinged room. Now she understood why the newspaper had said "rooms," for this was an old suite and here was the parlor. There was another, larger and older desk, a couch with a table in front, and with easy chairs on either side. The tall windows looked out on a parking lot in the rear. Maggie wondered if maybe, back then, it had been a garden. . . .

She could almost see it. Shading trees, tables with umbrellas sticking through the tops, slatted wooden armchairs. He might have taken his tea out there—who would have served him while he sat there—or here—dreaming up his tower?

She moved around the room slowly and then sat down on the couch. From here he'd caused the tower to be built. Had he gone out each day from this room to watch its growth?

She closed her eyes and tried to feel what he had felt, see what he had seen. She could see the tower rising stone by stone—but when she reached the top her imagination vanished. Nothing came to her about *why*—why he'd started, why he'd stopped.

She didn't feel anything about whether Mr. Miguel Sanchez Oliver St. James was alive or dead.

What an odd, almost disturbing name! She was glad she hadn't told Jimmy or Tom or Serena.

Oh, she wished she could sense something about him! But the room didn't help. It had long ago lost all traces of the "crazy man."

Maybe it was because Maggie hadn't felt anything in the rooms that she began to have new thoughts as she walked back out to the dark hallway.

"Suppose he really was crazy?" she wondered.

"Suppose he built it, just like Jerry Forbes said, as a monument—a memorial—to some woman?"

Suppose her special feelings, Maggie's feelings, about the tower were only in herself, and it really was nothing more than a madman's whim? Then—would she care if it came down?

She stopped at the head of the stairs, thinking. Yes! Even if she had created the magic, she would care. They would all care, even so.

But having for the first time admitted the possibility of truth in the "crazy" story, Maggie felt more than ever that she *must* find out about Mr. St. James.

When she walked down the steps the clerk said, "See anything? Nothing to see, hm?"

And when she didn't answer, he called after her rather nastily, "Curiosity killed the cat, you know."

Maggie ran to the newspaper to see Jerry Forbes.

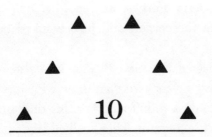

10

"Is there a way to find out for sure whether Mr. St. James is alive or dead?" she asked Jerry Forbes desperately.

He grabbed his straw hat from an old-fashioned tree that stood by the office partition. It had a feather band around it with a small fan of blue and yellow feathers poking up. He tapped it on his head jauntily, swung open the gate, and took Maggie's arm. They left the office together like that and went down the steps in rhythm.

Jerry said, in time with their echoing feet, "The tax collector, tax collector, tax collector ought to know. . . ."

Tax collector! How odd to feel so gay while going to see the tax collector. All her life Maggie had heard only bad things, growlings and ravings and grumblings, about the tax collector.

But here they were, and the sun was shining, and the round face of the town clock seemed to smile at them as they passed. In the shiny glass on the storefronts Maggie

saw the reflection of herself swinging down the street arm
in arm with Jerry Forbes. She couldn't help grinning at
the mirror on the corner, and Jerry winked back as they
marched past.

The office of the tax collector was also in the town
hall, and Maggie was very glad to be with Jerry. The lady
at the marble desk didn't stop her this time but looked at
them both with surprise. They walked right past, down a
long hall, to the office. Jerry pushed open the door, not
letting go of Maggie's arm, and marched in smiling.

"Want to see Mr. Meyers," said Jerry, so surely and
firmly, to the secretary, that she jumped up immediately
and disappeared behind a closed door.

A second later she poked her head out, "Who's calling?"

"Jerry Forbes of the Daily Express and Miss Margaret—" he looked at Maggie inquiringly.

"Amy," she whispered quickly, guessing he wanted
her middle name.

"Miss Margaret Amy Sanderson!"

My, it did sound impressive, called out that way!

They were ushered right in.

Mr. Meyers was fat. No, pudgy. No, rolled up
roundly, Maggie decided, all over. His cheeks were round
and his mouth was round, and so was his nose, and his
hands on the desk looked like a baby's.

He was like a series of buns glued together, thought
Maggie, and she nearly giggled aloud. There were even
round rolls above his eyebrows, and his shiny bald head,

with a sprinkle of pink from the sun, rolled back like a smooth round moon.

"Yes?" asked Mr. Meyers in a high skinny voice that wasn't at all like the rest of him.

In a pleasant but determined way, Jerry told him why they'd come. Mr. Meyers frowned, and it made the rolls over his eyebrows puff out.

"We consider the man to be dead," said Mr. Meyers in that funny high voice. "We've had no response to our letters—"

Jerry squeezed Maggie's arm—so Mr. Meyers did have an address!

"Notices have been placed in the paper with the same negative results—"

He sounded like a machine clicking out words, thought Maggie.

"Proper information about the property has been properly disseminated. If the man ignores his property and fails to pay due taxes, said property is duly forfeited according to the law. The matter is closed."

Then Jerry surprised Maggie. He became very stern and serious. "The matter can't be closed," he said. "And I'd like to know why, all over town, people are saying that the tower will come down. You can't know that in advance. The property hasn't been auctioned off yet."

"True," Mr. Meyers pursed his mouth out to a round cherry. "But whoever buys the lot will certainly take down the tower."

"How can you be sure of that?" insisted Jerry.

"Someone might buy the lot and keep the tower. Unless you already have an idea of the buyer. . . ."

Mr. Meyers smiled. "The lot will bring a fair price, beyond most people's reach I'm afraid. Property values have risen, but we do have a few interested parties."

Again Jerry squeezed Maggie's arm, and she understood. It shone from every inch of Mr. Meyers's round rolled face. He would outbid everyone else—he had already decided—and down would come the tower. Up would go—what? A house for Mr. Meyers? Oh, and if he were so determined to have the property, he'd never give them an address for Mr. St. James!

She made a small noise and Mr. Meyers looked at her, and then frowned at Jerry again. "Why are you interested in a man who's presumably dead?"

Jerry changed all over. In a twinkling he became a smiling, casual reporter. "Oh, the paper wants a story," he lied broadly. "And I'm helping this young lady do the same for the school paper."

"School paper?" Mr. Meyers was sharp underneath his round exterior. The school had never had a paper and he knew it.

Maggie hated to lie, but she felt she had to. "A paper *for* the school," she explained. "A—a story on—"

"On the crazy man and his tower," grinned Jerry. "Now that it's coming down everyone's interested. So goes the world! Up for a million years and nobody cares. Down, and people are curious. Human nature."

"Hm," said Mr. Meyers.

"It'll be good to see the tower go," said Jerry. "Time it came down. Nice to see something new there—improve the town altogether."

Comfortable and unsuspicious now, Mr. Meyers beamed at him. "Well—perhaps you could express those ideas in your story. And you, young lady," he smiled at Maggie, "in your report for school."

"Glad to, glad to!" Jerry stretched out his hand, and Mr. Meyers, rising like dough from his seat, shook it.

"By the way," Jerry added, pumping heartily, "I'd like to say what the crazy man's last known address was—in my story."

"Oh, there's no real address," smiled Mr. Meyers, flattered with Jerry's attention. "Never was. Just a post office box in the city."

"Do you recollect the number?" asked Jerry offhandedly. "People like numbers, you know. Superstitious about them. I could make something out of a number a crazy man would have—if it's a good one."

Mr. Meyers's eyes grew even rounder. "It was 757," he breathed.

"No!" Jerry stared at him. "Couldn't have been!"

"I ought to know," his round lips quivered. "Sent enough notices. 757 it was!"

"Wonderful!" Jerry whispered.

"Mean something?" warbled Mr. Meyers.

Jerry stared past Mr. Meyers's head, out the window.

"Couldn't be better," he intoned mysteriously. "Two sevens and a five! Oh, thank you, thank you very much!"

"Glad to be of service, very glad!"

"And *you*," Jerry nudged Maggie playfully, "if you want to know the meaning of those numbers, you'll have to look them up. I'm not going to tell you!"

He grinned at Mr. Meyers. "Can't give these kids everything. Gotta make 'em work, do research, *think*. Isn't that right?"

"Oh, yes indeed," said Mr. Meyers, as if Jerry was echoing everything he most deeply believed in. "Yes, *indeedy!*"

On that hearty, well-understood, everything-is-all-right, and we-are-all-together-in-this note, they parted.

Jerry took Maggie's arm and marched out as if he were going immediately, or even sooner, to pour himself over the typewriter and bring to life strange things about the number 757 to titillate readers of the Daily Express. And of course, to echo all of Mr. Meyers's sentiments about the tower. . . .

Maggie, so full of joy and laughter that she thought she might explode, waved back at the pudgy little tax collector.

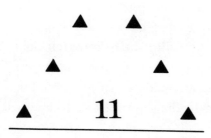

11

THEY MARCHED IN IDENTICAL RHYTHM PAST THE LADY OUT-side, whose head followed them in a slow, surprised movement, and tapped down the steps in front of the town hall. With upright backs and a posture of going-to-do-something, they paused at the corner and then crossed the street into the town hall park. With no destination, they marched as if they had one, up a path that first went straight, then curved, out of sight of the tax collector's window.

The moment they were out of his line of view, Jerry threw back his head and laughed. He removed his straw hat and tossed it high, high into the air.

(If Mr. Meyers had been watching from his window, he might have seen that jaunty hat sail high above the trees and float gaily down again.)

Jerry dashed to grab it as it barely missed getting hung on a branch. He plopped down on a bench and stuck his legs straight out and laughed all over, "What a time, what a time, what a time!"

Sitting beside him, Maggie crushed her hands between her knees, feeling that she wanted to jump and run all over—up the trees, across the grass, through the flower beds, everywhere. But she held herself tight and only her feet jiggled up and down on the cinder path. "You got the address!" she said, and her voice jumped with the excitement she was feeling—excited and happy, as she hadn't felt in years.

What a man," Jerry groaned happily. "What a peculiar man!"

"How old are you, Jerry?" Maggie asked suddenly.

Everything stopped as he stared at her with surprise. "Twenty-four. Why?"

"I wondered," said Maggie. And that was all there was to it, she had just wondered. "Maybe because I didn't know people could have such fun when they're—well—twenty-four."

"Ah! But what kind of fun, Maggie?" Jerry peered at her as if this were the most exciting question in the world. "It was fun, but why? Because he's such a funny, awful man? You did know I was lying, didn't you?"

"Oh, yes. About everything."

"Almost everything. Not everything. I didn't *start* by lying—remember?"

"I know," said Maggie.

"Do you realize, Miss Margaret Amy Sanderson," he laughed again, "that we went in with a simple, straightforward question and that that man caused us to lie? Why?"

He answered himself. "Because he's greedy and he's made some sort of a deal with his cronies, and he intends to buy that lot himself."

"I know." Maggie made circles in the cinder path with her toe. "And he'll take down the tower—but probably anybody would—and he'll put up a house."

"Maybe it'll be a fat, round, roly-poly house," muttered Jerry, and they laughed again.

"Or a thin, skinny one, like his voice," Maggie giggled.

"But the main thing is," said Jerry, "he'll be in it. That's what I think he intends to do. Build a new house for himself and rent his old one. Or vice versa. It's called going into real estate. Lots of people do it."

He turned to her with a blunt question. "You know, he may not be so horrible way deep down. Maybe he's got bad habits from being the tax collector. Would you really hate to have him live there so much? Are we being unfair?"

Are we being unfair? Never before had Maggie been asked such an important question. It was so simple, but it was real, and they were both involved in it, and she had been asked by a grown-up! (Or near grown-up. Jerry didn't seem that old.)

She was thrilled all over to be included in this question. It sang in her like a musical note. She looked at the trees, the cinder path, and the bed of pansies, and got goose pimples thinking to herself, "My first important question!"

The answer came out in an eleven-year-old way, but Maggie never forgot the effort. She visualized looking at Mr. Meyers every day, and at Mr. Meyers's house instead of the tower. . . .

"Maybe we are because . . . maybe he can't help being so fat and funny looking, and . . . there *are* greedy people, and maybe they can't help that, either."

She didn't want to answer like that, certainly not about Mr. Meyers. But maybe all important questions were like that. It gave Maggie a taste of the future—of the surprise when one touched one's own truth—and found what one didn't want to know.

"Maybe we are being unfair," she whispered.

"But he lied first," Jerry reminded her. "He suggested things. Suggested that everything was going straight according to law, and it isn't."

"Isn't it?"

"No." Jerry set his hat on the back of his head. "The law says that anyone has a chance at an auction, but somehow he has it all sewn up in advance. He has some scheme, maybe to start the bidding too high, so it'll be too expensive for ordinary folks," he grinned at her, "like you and me. And he's already got some understanding with his friends, who could afford it, to let him have it. No, it's not according to law, really. And that," he added, "is why I don't like him."

"I don't like him either," said Maggie. And that simple statement, was, in its own way, as great a truth as the other she'd found.

"So are you going to write to that post office box?" asked Jerry.

"Number 757," said Maggie, beginning to smile.

"The most mysterious number in the world!" Jerry grinned.

"The death number," murmured Maggie.

"Maybe the death-defying number!" said Jerry. "Listen, Maggie Sanderson—*write*! You'd better, after what I went through to get that number for you!"

"He never answered Mr. Meyers," said Maggie.

"But if he's alive, he might answer you!"

When they parted on the other side of the park, Maggie walked toward home on the balls of her feet, not letting her heels touch the ground. She wanted to feel that springy thrust that tipped her forward—going somewhere with something to do. It was a deep-down bubbling something, around a point of seriousness—the tower—but included the gaiety and joy of an afternoon with Jerry Forbes.

She subtracted eleven from twenty-four and found thirteen. When she was eighteen he'd be thirty-one. No, when she was twenty he'd be thirty-three. Twenty-one, and he'd be thirty-four . . . was that too great a distance?

She was deep in dreams about herself and Jerry Forbes, or someone just like Jerry, when she crossed a street, tipping forward, and ran into her teacher.

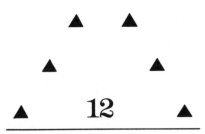

12

"Maggie, almost everyone else has brought in their part of the map," said Miss Wiley. "How nice to see you."

"Hello," said Maggie, coming down hard on her heels.

Miss Wiley looked more like an owl than ever, for she was wearing a gray dress with a cape and her hair was frizzed up like feathers.

"Do bring it in Monday," said her teacher. "You must learn to finish things, Maggie."

"I know. I'm sorry I'm late."

"And I gave you the most interesting part to do. England is such fun! All those fascinating cathedrals—one would be so nice on the map, don't you think? Although of course it needn't be. Oh, I wish I were in a school again and had a chance to do this! You could do a palace or a boat on the river Thames. I'd love to see a monarch—or Stonehenge! Those wonderful stones. I remember you liked them, Maggie.

"And it would be so dreary," Miss Wiley ended breathlessly, "to have a map without any figures on it at all!"

She sounded, in speaking about England, as if she'd just returned from there herself, thought Maggie. Of course all this bright, breathless, informative nagging was to interest Maggie, an effort to get her to complete her part.

"I'll try to do it this weekend," said Maggie.

"Fine!" Miss Wiley beamed. Her blue eyes behind the glasses were so huge they looked like robins' eggs. "And have a lovely weekend. It gives such a good feeling, Maggie, to finish something. Wait until you see our map all across the wall."

She waved and tripped on across the street in her high-heeled gray shoes that matched the dress. She should have flown, flapping the cape, Maggie thought, at the same time wishing that she didn't always see her teacher as a large gray bird!

She liked Miss Wiley, who was the most popular teacher in school, and the most modern. And she appreciated her interest. "I will do it," Maggie promised herself. "I will finish it. Just to make Miss Wiley happy."

Serena and Tom and Jimmy knew she'd been somewhere when she turned into the street. They came running from Tom's front lawn and leaned over the fence.

"Did you find out anything?"

"I got a post office box number," said Maggie.

"How?"

"Well—," Maggie hesitated. "In an office," she said quickly, "and it's his last address and I'm going to write to him."

"Isn't he dead?" asked Serena.

"Nobody knows."

"What will you say?" asked Tom.

"I don't know."

"Make it good," said Jimmy, "or he won't even answer you."

"He probably can't," said Tom. "It's probably the dead letter box!"

The boys laughed and Serena said, "Do you want us all to sign our names to the letter, Maggie?"

Maggie loved Serena for that!

Tom said, "Oh, that'd be silly if he's dead."

"If my parents found out I'd signed a letter," Jimmy added, "I'd be in trouble. They want the tower to come down."

"Everybody does," said Tom, and they all became quiet thinking about that.

"Maybe I'd better just sign my name," said Maggie. "I don't mind."

"Well—," said Tom.

"Well—," said Jimmy.

"Are you sure, Maggie?" Serena asked.

They seemed to feel she was being very brave.

"Well, I don't see how anyone could find out anyway," she said. "But even if they did, I wouldn't care. About being blamed, I mean. One person's better than four."

"Where's the post office box?" asked Jimmy.

"In the city."

"The city!" They hung over the fence staring at Maggie.

The city was so far away. Most of them had never been there. Their parents said it was too expensive to visit. It was big and shiny and unknown . . . more unknown to them, in fact, than Europe and all the faraway countries they studied about in school. The city! Maybe nobody answered letters sent to the city. Maybe it was so big that letters got lost.

"I'm going to write!" said Maggie firmly, reading all the questions in their faces.

And for all that day and the next she didn't do a bit of work on her map for Miss Wiley. Instead she wrote on piece after piece of paper, discarding them in the trash basket. "Dear Mr. St. James. Dear Mr. Miguel St. James. Dear Mr. Oliver St. James. . . ." She didn't know which to use.

But she wrote him a five-page letter. Then a four-page letter. Then three pages, and two, and one . . . and threw them all away.

Finally she wrote: "Dear Mr. St. James, I would like to see you about the tower."

She signed her name and took it to the store to get a

stamp. The small grocery store where they shopped had stamps and there was a mailbox right outside, between the sidewalk and the street. Maggie looked at it for a long time. It was blue, and had a great rounded top; a notice was posted on it about the time of pick-ups. A flag of the United States was painted on the top, and it was all made of heavy iron and looked as if it swallowed everything up.

Once inside, the letter would never come out, even if she changed her mind.

Maggie walked up and down a crack in the sidewalk. Small leaves and bits of grass were scattered over the cement squares, and from the tree above, yellow pollen came drifting down. She heard bees buzzing overhead.

Finally she stepped from the sidewalk to the grass and lifted the iron handle and raised the letter slot, and let the letter slide, ever so slowly, from her hand. It drifted down somewhere inside and didn't make a sound.

She didn't go home right away but stood there wondering if she had written the right thing. Bees began buzzing around her short brown hair, and ants crawled up on her short white socks. Finally the mailman came, humming, and didn't seem to notice her at all. She was a statue, standing on the grass.

He unlocked the mailbox and swept out a great pile of envelopes with brightly colored stamps. He shoved them all into an immense green canvas bag which he swung over his shoulder, and then marched away, still humming.

"Dear Mr. St. James—." Her words were gone, carried away.

Maggie shivered in the warm sun and turned homeward. The eyes of the tower looked at her and she wondered if the tower even remembered Mr. St. James? Maybe now it only knew her.

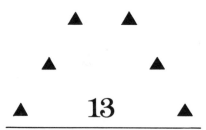

13

FOR ALL THE NEXT WEEK NO ANSWER CAME TO MAGGIE'S letter. She could think of nothing but that, so she was the last person in class to bring in her part of the map. The rest of medieval Europe reached across the classroom wall, quite beautiful and colorful, with only the lower part of the British Isles missing.

Miss Wiley stopped asking Maggie about it, and only looked at her. Maggie became superstitious, thinking, "Maybe if I finish the map a letter will come."

So finally she did it on the sheet of heavy paper she'd taken home, coloring it carefully, and did a detailed drawing of Westminster Abbey that she copied from her textbook. When it was finally in place, everyone clapped.

"How beautiful, Maggie!" Miss Wiley exclaimed.

The children were really surprised at her work.

And Miss Wiley, adding, "You finished it!" glowed rosily all over. She thought that Maggie had broken through something that impeded her.

But still no answer came.

Maggie looked at all the unfinished things in her room and wondered: if she set to work industriously and completed everything, would that bring her an answer? She looked out her window at the tower and decided—no! They must remain unfinished or the tower would fall. She then became superstitious and began to leave little unfinished ends on everything—one dish unwashed, one corner unswept—until she decided that was silly, too.

She talked out her window to the tower, asking it questions: "Why are you so important to me?" And then she added, "To us," thinking of Jimmy and Tom and Serena. "We don't want you not to be there. Can't you help bring me an answer? Or tell us how to keep you?"

And many times during the first week of waiting, and then the next, Maggie went alone to the tower and climbed to the top, running her hand over the blistered rail, looking up at the charred peak, and around at the walls of stone. A faint scent of smoke and ash still lingered.

She began to wonder a new thing: if the peak were finished, if the whole spire was constructed, would people still want it to come down?

Serena and Tom and Jimmy were getting the same idea.

"Maybe we could finish it," they said. "Maybe we could put a real peak on the top."

"How could we do it?"

"With wood?"

"With stones?"

"Maybe with big pieces of cardboard?"

They sighed, seeing the impossibility. The tower was high and hard for them to finish, as they were neither carpenters nor stonemasons; they had no ladders or scaffolding. . . .

"But anyway," Maggie said, "if we could do it, we'd just be doing it for other people. Would you . . . would you *like* it if it were finished like that?"

There was a long silence before Jimmy said, first, "No."

Tom echoed him, "Hm, hm," and Serena shook her head, saying, "I wouldn't."

"Why not?" asked Maggie.

They puzzled over that, and Tom said, "Well, then it would be just . . . ordinary, sort of."

"Yeah," said Jimmy. "And this way, unfinished, it's— it's better. More mysterious."

"It lets me pretend about things," said Serena. "Any other way, it just wouldn't be the same," and the boys nodded in agreement.

Every day Maggie looked in the mailbox and every day there was nothing.

Then suddenly, school was over for the term. There was a party on the last day, and afterward the children left their classrooms, whooping and hollering and running

wild down the streets. They flapped their arms and made
great wild leaps, throwing themselves to the summer, to
the freedom of the warm sun and fields and brooks, and to
swimming and fishing and bicycling under the wide, shading trees.

Maggie's mother became so ill with the heat that she
took to her bed and even the doctor came. Maggie was
frightened when she heard his report—it was heat exhaus-
tion, but he was also concerned about her blood pressure,
and her heart.

"Eat less," he told her firmly. "And drink more fluids
and take salt pills. And, Mrs. Sanderson, when you're able,
you must get more exercise." He snapped shut his black
bag and tipped his hat to Maggie and her father when he
left.

They were both frightened, even though the doctor
had said it was nothing to worry about yet, as long as she
was careful, and most importantly, lost weight.

They made a bed for her on the couch in the parlor.
Maggie placed her slippers neatly beside the couch, and
then opened every window. She pulled back the drapes
and shoved the glass curtains aside. The couch faced the
open kitchen door, so Maggie drew back the kitchen curtains, too, and soon a pleasant cross breeze began to drift
through the house.

Still her mother complained, "It's so hot!"

So Maggie's father bought water-cooled fans and set
them around the parlor. He got home earlier now each

day, and checked the jar of ice water and the salt pills, and hovered about, offering iced coffee and tea.

Maggie did most of the cooking and all of the shopping, and made sure there were no heavy roasts or potatoes. Whenever she went to the store she felt her mother's life was in her hands.

From the couch, Mrs. Sanderson could see the tower through the kitchen windows, and at first she seemed to find it an unpleasant sight. "Ugly that is, so ugly. I wish they'd take it down soon," she would murmur, and turn her face away.

But she also saw it at night when she couldn't sleep. And she watched the moon rise behind it. Once, when Maggie came downstairs, she found her mother awake in the dark, staring out at the peak that was bathed in moonlight. She seemed to have forgotten her heavy, panting body. Her face was different—relaxed—and she didn't breathe so swiftly.

Maggie didn't disturb her. She didn't walk through to the kitchen for the glass of juice she'd come down for. Instead she tiptoed upstairs and looked out her own window for a long time. . . .

Was her mother frightened, too? She never said a word; she just accepted everything placidly. But the sight of the peak, pointing to the stars, seemed to help, even to reassure her. . . .

Suppose her mother died? Maggie's throat tightened and she choked back tears. But she couldn't die! The doctor had said she wouldn't. And if her mother were frightened, she would never say so.

Maggie whispered to the tower, "Thank you for helping her."

Her father drew her aside one day, because he had to confide in someone, because he couldn't keep it to himself any longer. "Maggie, I'm terribly worried about your mother."

"She's a little better now, but she needs more exercise. She needs to walk!" said Maggie, so earnestly, so seriously, that her father's face grew grave with thought.

The next day he made her get up for a while. The whole family took a slow ride out to the lake, and Maggie brought along a box lunch. They sat at the water's edge, looking at rowboats, eating tiny sandwiches. Maggie had deliberately made them thin. Her mother walked for a short distance along the shore, and when the afternoon was over, she seemed a lot better.

But that night the weather turned sullen and humid and pressed down on everyone in town. There was no moon, nor wind, nor air, but only huge, oppressive clouds overhead, and everything was damp and sticky. Maggie's mother lay panting and fanning herself, and, even with the fans, could get no relief.

She seemed to be watching the tower—watching *for* the tower now, thought Maggie. And when the storm finally broke in great clapping crashes of thunder, and the cooling rain came in a downpour, and then a wind came that pushed the clouds away, so the tower appeared again —her mother saw it from the couch and smiled.

Maggie went to her room and wrote another letter to Mr. St. James. She didn't struggle to think of something new to say; she wrote the same thing she had before, but added, "Please. *Please!*"

And she shook the envelope at the tower before she mailed it. "Make him answer. You make him answer!"

And five days later a letter came.

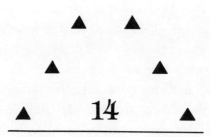

14

Maggie's mother had lost quite a bit of weight by the time the doctor came again. He said it was wonderful and very good for her. If she kept right on with her diet and exercise there was nothing to worry about. Maggie was so relieved that she cried.

Her mother began to move about a little more and worked in the kitchen now and then. So she was up and standing by the door when Maggie went for the mail that day. The little red box stood on a pole by their gate, and the flag was up. Letters were very rare, but it was time for the monthly bills.

At first, when Maggie pulled out three envelopes, she thought they were all bills. There was one for water, one for electricity, and the third envelope was large and white and typed just like business mail. It took her a moment to realize that it was actually addressed to Miss Margaret Sanderson.

"What's there, Maggie?" her mother called.

"Bills!" She faced away from the house and stuffed the letter down the neck of her dress. It made a crinkling sound against her chest as she walked in and handed the other mail to her mother.

She pressed her hand against her dress to keep it quiet and ran upstairs, quivering. Her father was at work, her mother was downstairs and busy, but Maggie had an illogical fear that she might be found with the letter and interrupted while reading it.

The bathroom! She could lock the door. No, it wasn't right. Her closet! Nobody would find her in there. No! She could just close the door to her room.

She did, and sat down on the edge of her bed and tore open the letter. She didn't even look at the return address. If she had, she would have seen there was none. The paper was all wrinkled now from the hasty way she'd stuffed it down her dress, and she had to smooth out the creases before she read.

> *Dear Miss Sanderson,*
> *You may speak about the tower. Allow five hours*
> *Thursday, One P.M., Hotel Imperial.*
> *Yours very truly,*
A. O. Chalcot
(M.S.O.S.J.)

A shiver rushed up Maggie's spine, tickled her shoulder blades and lingered at the back of her neck. She glanced out at the tower and the shiver returned, spread-

ing down from her shoulders to her legs. She went goose-
pimply all over. She read the letter again, and reread it,
smoothing out the creases, over and over, on her lap.

It was, oh, infinitely more mysterious than anything
she had imagined! The hotel. Five hours. Speak about the
tower . . . her heart beat wildly. Maybe this was the way
her mother had felt when she couldn't breathe properly.

What could she say for five hours? And to whom?

Who was Chalcot? Why were Mr. St. James's initials
put in below like that? Five hours! What could she say?
She had exactly one thing to say and it would take . . .
Maggie counted, saying it aloud to herself . . . exactly six
seconds.

"We want to keep the tower."

If you counted "Tower" as two seconds, it would take
seven seconds to say it. *Five hours!* Maybe she wouldn't
be able to speak at all.

Should she tell Serena and Jimmy and Tom? Or Jerry
Forbes? Could they help? What would they say? Could
they tell her something to say? Or would they have as
many questions about this as she did?

Her head began to buzz. She wouldn't be able to
stand all their questions on top of hers. She'd be stuffed,
so tongue-tied that she wouldn't be able to utter a sound
on Thursday.

Thursday! This was Tuesday!

How did it go? "Monday's child is fair of face, Tuesday's child is full of grace, Wednesday's child is. . . ." Was

it "full of woe or far to go"? She couldn't remember! She repeated it again, fast, and thought it was "Thursday's child has far to go."

Far to go! Yes, the Hotel Imperial now seemed as distant as the moon, and so did the time stretching from now until Thursday. Maggie began to tremble and kept on trembling. Everything was so mixed up within her that she couldn't sort it all out. Was Mr. St. James alive or dead? Who was A. O. Chalcot?

Why did they—or he—demand five hours from her? The letter itself seemed like a demand of some sort. . . .

But she was the one who had started this. It was only a reply to her own letter. She looked at the tower for help, but it was distant now, almost unknown. It stared back with empty, unhelpful eyes.

Maggie remained nervous all that day, with a low, slow, continual shaking deep inside. It was a little like the way she felt before appearing in school plays, only worse. There were *scripts* for plays! And a play didn't last five hours!

She stayed indoors, avoiding Serena and the boys. She didn't know what to tell them, if anything, and she was afraid they might read something in her eyes.

She moved aimlessly around upstairs, wishing she had something definite to do. She looked into her mother's and father's bedroom, but everything was neat. The high old bed, the bureau with silver-framed photos of her grandparents, next to the tortoise-shell brush and comb set. . . .

Maybe A. O. Chalcot was a lawyer! The initials below could mean that Mr. St. James was dead, and that Chalcot was merely answering for him. Or, Chalcot could be connected with the town—even with the tax collector's office!

A. O. Chalcot could be a woman, Maggie suddenly realized. Maybe Mr. St. James had a daughter, married to someone named Chalcot . . . but then wouldn't she have signed it "Mrs."?

Oh, why hadn't there been more explanation!

Maggie roamed out in the hall, looking for something to do again. Everything was clean. She looked into the bathroom. The windows had curtains with an ugly design of circles and squares pushed together. Maggie stood there looking at them blankly, not seeing them.

Once her class had been pen pals, she remembered, with other children who lived far away. Maggie had received a letter all the way from Canada. The little girl had described high mountains covered with forests, and colorful totem poles and canoes. She lived in the northwest, near those Indian things. Maggie had gazed at the stamp from British Columbia and fingered the letter as if it could give her the smell of those forests and the ocean. She had felt how strange it was to get a letter from so far away.

But that wasn't half so strange, hadn't felt nearly as far away as this short, abrupt note.

Maybe they wouldn't even know it was just a little girl who'd written to them! They might be expecting a grown woman! Could they—or he—tell just by her hand-writing?

She looked behind the curtains to see if the bathroom windows needed washing. They were clean, but there were some drips of old paint around the frames. She got a razor blade out of the cabinet and spent the afternoon there, carefully and patiently scraping off each small fleck.

But the nervousness stayed with her all that day and Maggie came to Wednesday in the same way.

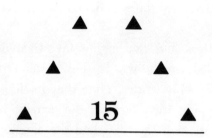

15

On Wednesday there came several sets of visitors to the tower.

First came Mr. Meyers, who rolled up in a large, open car with several other expensively dressed gentlemen. They wore neat business suits and Mr. Meyers looked like a small fat apple bobbing alongside them. They left the car noisily, slamming the doors, speaking with loud voices, and stamped across the sidewalk to march through the weeds to the tower.

They went round it, peered at it, felt the huge gray stones, stood at the four corners, and squinted at the lot as if they were taking measure. All the time they kept calling to each other.

The children and almost all the neighbors were outside their homes, observing. The men seemed to enjoy this silent audience, and their laughter and talk and gestures got louder and loftier and wider. They all disappeared inside the tower for a while and Maggie could hear Mr.

Meyers's voice rise beyond the rest. It seemed to pipe out like a thin, squeaky flute, and float from the top of the tower.

When they had thoroughly investigated the tower and tramped down the weeds, they marched back to the car with high, wide strides. Then they made a great business of stamping their feet on the cement to shake off earth and dust, and then brushed the clinging weeds off their trouser legs, and wiped their shoes carefully on the sidewalk edge.

They paused then, like actors at a curtain call, and postured around the car, lighting cigars, with elaborate gestures. They were very careful to notice no one but each other, to take no regard of neighbors looking on. When cigars were successfully lit, they whipped open the car doors and made another great to-do of "After you, after *you*!" Bowing, ushering, waving arms to the seats, one by one they got in and settled down heavily. They leaned back their heads, cigars tipped up, and smoke drifted up to the sky.

Mr. Meyers sat in front, next to the door. He flicked his ash over the side, with a pudgy, impatient hand, and smiled at the tower as the car sped off with an important-sounding roar.

Maggie remembered her conversation with Jerry Forbes as clearly as if it were taking place *now* . . . "Are we being unfair?" Still, she would have given almost anything for a rubber band and a tack!

One lovely sharp-pointed tack to speed like the wind from a well-aimed rubber band. Pop! Woosh! Right at that sinister-looking rear tire. And so much for Mr. Meyers!

"What was all that, Maggie?" her mother called from inside the house. She'd been lying down and was probably the only woman in the neighborhood who hadn't been a witness.

"Some men," Maggie called back from the porch. "And the man who's going to buy the tower."

She heard her mother say, "Oh," faintly, without questioning it, and that bothered her.

Tom and Jimmy and Serena came running to the fence and beckoned to her. "Did you see all those men?"

Maggie crossed the lawn, nervous again. For a minute, thinking about the tack, she'd felt better, and had almost forgotten about the letter. Now what should she say? Should she tell them anything? Oh, she wished she'd stayed inside and watched from her window.

"Looking at the tower like that," cried Tom. "Maybe it means they'll hold an auction soon."

"One of them may buy it!" said Jimmy, sounding disturbed. "And you didn't get an answer to your letter."

"Why don't you write again?" pleaded Tom.

"Or tell us what the box number is, and we'll all write," said Serena.

Maggie felt awful. She was bursting to tell them that she *had* written again. They only knew she'd written once.

She itched to say that she had received an answer, and that she had an appointment—tomorrow! But she felt something in the letter that seemed to beg for silence.

And . . . they changed so often, Serena and Jimmy and Tom. They were like the wind that rose and came down again. One minute they were like this, reaching her heart, serious about serious things, and the next moment they might go way up, out of her reach—silly—and start joking.

She couldn't tell if they could be responsible, and if she could trust them to stay with her, and not change, and remember to be serious. She could never go to that appointment if they started joking!

And if they went wild and told somebody—if they mentioned it to a single soul—she'd never be able to go. Gossip moved around the neighborhood; Tom and Jimmy liked to brag, and Serena loved leaving mysterious hints in the air.

As much as it hurt, as much as she longed to include them, Maggie remained silent about the letter. She only said, in a vague manner, "Let's just wait a day or so—maybe something will happen. And if it doesn't," she added, "well, then you can all write."

They couldn't pry the box number from her that Wednesday morning.

Later, as one thing leads to another, as if a whisper had rustled through town, the second set of visitors flocked to the tower. Cars drove through the street that had never been seen there before. Lines of them crept down the block, while curious heads turned to stare. And later in the afternoon, following the cars, appeared a group of older boys from another part of town who liked to gang and roam together.

They came in a huge bunch, like many grapes on one stem, moving slowly, and then they broke off, one by one, to circle the tower. Laughing and jeering, they examined the high gray walls and open windows. They began to pick up pebbles from under the weeds, and, lightly at first, aimed them through the windows. Some fell through, but others hit the stone walls, and then the boys began to throw them recklessly.

Then fiercely. Larger and larger stones crashed, banged, ricocheted, as they picked up more and more and flailed the tower with a rain of flying stones. Their arms whipped the air harder and harder . . . until one boy himself was hit on the head by a flying rock, and blood welled from his forehead. The rest gathered around to shield him, as if he were something unseemly. They bunched together again in that peculiar shape and moved off in one sullen, growling body.

The tower withstood the attack, standing firm, gray, and silent, in the warm afternoon. The ground below was littered with pebbles and stones, and grass and weeds were flattened and broken from tramping feet.

But all of this, it seemed, was only a small display of the townspeople's odd feelings. For during the night, when all the neighborhood was fast asleep, others came.

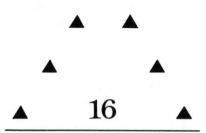

16

When Maggie awoke Thursday morning—Thursday! the Day!—she found the tower disfigured.

They had come in the night to scrawl all over it in chalk and crayon and paint. Names were written on it, and slogans, and rude remarks about the crazy man. All over, as high as arms could reach, were strings of vile words and oaths. They had used the tower as a depository for all the things one didn't say aloud, for all the feelings one didn't outwardly express.

It was so early in the morning that the birds were barely awake. Maggie stood at her window and saw all the horrible things on the tower—but she then saw something else.

Tom and Jimmy were walking across the lot with buckets of soapy water and stiff brushes; and a minute later Serena flew from her house to help. Maggie ran down, too. Together, almost silently, they worked in the cool morning, their legs and feet wet from dew still on the

grass. They threw on soapy water and washed and
scrubbed the walls until their arms ached.

Serena looked as if she wanted to cry, and Tom and
Jimmy looked furious.

Now more than ever Maggie wanted to tell them
about today, where she was going, and when. But as she
worked on the stone walls, the tower itself seemed to cau-
tion her to be silent. And they were all strangely silent,
working together.

As the neighbors around woke up, and men drove off
to work and women came out of their houses, they noticed
the children working, and saw what had been done to the
tower. They frowned at first, at the ugly words, then
smiled at the children, because cleaning off the words
seemed such a decent thing to do, and then they shook
their heads in wonder. The tower wouldn't be there much
longer. Children working so hard in the summer was a
puzzling thing to see. . . .

"That's all, I guess," said Jimmy, finally.

"As much as we can do," said Tom.

"I'll ask my father if he can help where we haven't
been able to reach," Serena offered.

Maggie, who had to give them *something*, some word
now, said, "You know, I have a feeling! Maybe something
will happen today!"

Later she was very glad she hadn't said more. She
became very nervous again as the hours marched toward
one o'clock. The morning's work had helped, though, and

the trembling had collected itself into a small, compact place in the pit of her stomach. If she were lucky, it would stay there and leave her head free to speak for the tower, to speak for *all* of them.

At twelve o'clock she stood in front of her mirror, dressed carefully in a brown jumper, a white blouse, and her good brown school shoes. She brushed her hair hard, as if her hand were already expressing the things she wished she could say about the tower. When she finished, her hair framed her face like a short cap of thick brown silk. She squeezed her eyes, wishing they were closer together, and then looked at them separately, one eye at a time, to like herself more.

But Maggie thought she looked very small and unimportant, like a small, brown nervous animal. . . .

"Where are you going, Maggie?" her mother asked, surprised to see her come downstairs so neatly dressed up.

"To meet Miss Wiley at the library," Maggie lied. "It's a special thing for the summer. . . ." She hated to lie like this! But she could never tell her mother she was really going to the Hotel Imperial, or why. She'd be kept in the house.

"I won't be back until six. Is that all right?"

"You didn't say anything about it before," her mother complained.

"I'm sorry."

"Oh—I'll be all right," her mother finally smiled. "You go along and have a good time."

That made Maggie feel even worse. But the guilt about lying made her nervousness subside. One thing added on to the other gave her a more normal feeling as she walked out of the house to meet "Chalcot"—or whoever it was she would meet.

The other children didn't see her leave, and on her way downtown, she didn't pass anyone she knew. It was odd, Maggie reflected, that she hadn't felt she could tell even Jerry Forbes about this. Later . . . maybe later, she would . . . after she told Serena and Tom and Jimmy.

At one minute to one she edged around the corner of the block to the hotel entrance. She had walked around the block once, then twice again. The letter had been so precise about time that Maggie felt she must be equally precise. She felt limp and empty-headed, though, and sort of numb.

So much tension of anticipation, so much curiosity, so many questions, had left her with nothing but enough energy to move her feet along.

The sun was glaring off the yellow shingles of the Hotel Imperial when she stepped into the lobby. It was cool there, out of the sun. She didn't even glance at the man behind the desk, but headed straight for the stairs.

"Where do you think you're going?" he called out.

She stopped and looked at him. It wasn't the same black-haired man. This one was old, with frizzy gray hair and a drooping, suspicious face. She didn't know what to say, and she was abruptly very nervous again. Should she tell him that Mr. St. James, or Chalcot, or someone, was waiting for her in suite number 27? Should she ask this man to "announce" her? Had someone left word to expect her? Should she give him her name?

It never occurred to Maggie that this meeting would take place anywhere than in Mr. St. James's old rooms.

"Where do you think you're going?" the man repeated angrily as Maggie hung there, undecided on what to say.

Then, through the glass doors leading to the street, she saw the long black limousine pull up in front of the hotel. It was the same car that had visited the tower last year, with the same man in a chauffeur's cap seated behind the wheel. Her eyes traveled to the clock behind the desk. Exactly one o'clock!

Quickly, Maggie darted out of the lobby to the sidewalk and stood beside the car. Her heart was pounding hard. Who would get out? The gray curtains covered all the rear windows inside, just as they had last year. . . .

The chauffeur leaned over to ask her out the open window, "Good afternoon, Miss Sanderson?"

"Yes," Maggie whispered.

He nodded and smiled. He didn't seem at all surprised to see that she was just a little girl!

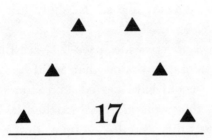

17

"Yes, we were expecting you," the chauffeur smiled, getting out of the car. "You are very prompt."

He came around to the sidewalk and inclined his head toward Maggie. It was almost like a bow.

"It is a two-hour drive to the city and the same time back again," he said. "That will leave you one hour for your discussion."

The city!

Maggie gaped, too surprised to speak. But she felt so *stupid* not to have thought of it! Of course! The note meant only to meet at the Hotel Imperial—not to speak there for *five* hours! But only *one*! In the city! Her knees went weak with relief, but she had never felt quite so small or embarrassed by all her imagination.

The chauffeur smiled at her obvious surprise and asked politely, "I hope you managed to arrange the time?"

Breathlessly, Maggie nodded, and he opened the rear

door for her, then took his place behind the wheel and drove smoothly away. She sat carefully in the luxurious limousine.

There was a very wide space between them, divided by a partition and a window that could be moved up or down. If she could have moved, and stretched her legs straight out, they wouldn't have reached halfway to the two small seats that were folded up against the partition. Everything was of shiny, navy-blue leather, with gold fittings.

The driver smiled at her through his mirror as she took it all in, and he drove very carefully, very smoothly. Finally, when there was a glimpse of trees and open spaces outside the town, he said, "You may open the curtains now, Miss Sanderson."

It was the first movement Maggie had made. It felt funny to move her hands up to pull aside the soft gray curtains.

"All around if you like," he said, and she did, feeling better as she turned her body to push them back from the rear window, and reached over to the window on her left as well.

The car filled with light, and the sunshine made a hot pool on the leather seat. They were well out of town now, on the highway, passing fields and barns and patches of forest. They sped past grazing cows and horses running behind white fences. Farmers with tractors moved slowly, like dots in the distance.

Maggie's first real thought was, "What would Serena and Tom and Jimmy think!"

It was so fantastic, so impossible, that it almost wasn't real! The city! She'd never been to the city. And neither had they. And to go in a—a limousine like this! They would never believe it! "Thursday's child has far to go. . . ." She shivered and became nervous again.

"One hour for your discussion," the chauffeur had said. That wasn't nearly as bad as five—but still, what could she say? Should she ask *him* about it? But if he had only been sent to drive her to the city and back, he might not even know why. Probably chauffeurs just went where they were told to go and never knew why. . . .

But he seemed . . . different somehow, thought Maggie. He gave such soft suggestions—or directions. She looked at him curiously, finally noticing that he wasn't a young man. He was middle-aged at least, and it was just his voice that sounded young. It also sounded slightly foreign—just a little. He had a handsome, almost classical face, of a light almond color, and gray-green eyes. His gentle smile said that he was a nice man—but different. He looked different from anyone she'd ever seen before.

"This is beautiful country," he reminded her, as if asking Maggie not to stare so curiously at his reflection in the mirror, and to pay more attention to the world outside.

She did, gazing out at the gently rising and falling land. The car went fast now, but so smoothly that she felt that the world was moving away, not they over the world. Little by little Maggie relaxed until she finally felt she could say something.

"I've—I've never been to the city."

"Hm, hm," he nodded, as if he already knew that.

Then she managed to ask what she really wanted. "Mr. St. James—is he really alive?"

The chauffeur was silent for some time before answering, "He is very old."

Maggie caught her breath. Alive, then! He was alive! Now all her questions wanted to bubble out. Would she see him, then, or Chalcot! And who was Chalcot? And how old was Mr. St. James?

"He doesn't travel anymore," the driver added, and there was something final in his tone, something that told Maggie to wait. She would learn everything in time.

Perhaps he wasn't allowed to talk about his employer. He didn't say another word, and there wasn't a sound inside the car except for the hum of the motor. . . .

"He is very old. He doesn't travel anymore." With those few words he had explained that Mr. St. James couldn't have made another trip to Maggie's town. He must have come to look at the tower for the last time a year ago. Was he ill now, as well as old? What could she say to a very old and ill man about the tower?

And what would he say to her! What if she had done all this and come this far only to hear that he didn't care about it anymore? What if he wanted it to come down and just thought it would be proper, after her letters, to tell her?

And suppose she learned that he *had* built it for a silly reason, that it didn't contain a secret, didn't mean anything, and wasn't mysterious at all? Could she persuade him differently, and explain that it still meant something and was important to her and the other children?

She couldn't think! The effort made her head ache, and the motion of the smoothly rolling car made her sleepy. She didn't fall asleep, but gazed out the window in a sort of trance for the rest of the drive. They stopped once at a gas station and Maggie used the ladies' room. She felt very odd under the stares of the attendant when the chauffeur opened the car door for her. He must have thought she was very special, like one of Serena's princesses, and all Maggie could think of was her father's old, shabby car.

They drove on and Maggie watched the land, saw the beginnings of clusters of houses, and then saw factories on the outskirts of the city. Smoke trailed in long feathers across the sky. They began to stop more frequently at traffic lights.

Maggie sat up straight, tense again, now that the moment was near. Two hours had passed, and she had scarcely been aware of time. Even the city, now that she saw part of it, didn't interest her. It looked bleak and depressing so far, not shiny and exciting and wonderful as people said. All of her attention was on the coming hour.

"Would you please close the curtains again now, Miss Sanderson?" the driver asked.

Maggie did so, as he added softly, "It is just that there are so many unnecessary gossipings in all towns and cities."

The car turned right and left down many streets and finally drew up to a curb. Maggie started to reach for the door handle but then remembered to wait until it was opened for her. As she got out, the chauffeur reminded her again, "Mr. St. James is very old."

They were in front of a house of red stone with a flight of steps leading up to huge windows with double wooden doors. On either side of the doors were high windows with fan-shaped tops. Two stone dragons with their tails curled over the balustrades sat at the top of the steps. The driver locked the car and they walked up to a massive bronze knocker shaped like two coiling snakes.

Maggie thought the driver would use it, or ring the bell she saw to one side, but instead he took a key from his pocket and unlocked the door. He held it open for Maggie and stood back, ushering her in. She walked into a dark hall where he took off his cap, bowed to Maggie, and said, "One moment, please."

Opening a door off the hall, he disappeared inside, closing it softly behind him. Maggie looked around, but it was very dark after the sun outside, and before her eyes adjusted, the chauffeur opened the door wide and motioned to her.

She walked into a great, high-ceilinged room that gave an impression of vast spaciousness although it was filled with objects. She couldn't immediately take it all in, but there were hangings and paintings and carved chests and statues. . . .

And in a deep chair, holding out a hand to greet her, she saw Miguel Sanchez Oliver St. James.

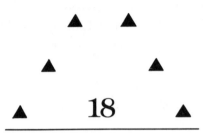

18

OH, HE WAS SO OLD! SO OLD THAT MAGGIE COULDN'T SEE what he had once been. His old head nodded and trembled; his face was rippled with wrinkles. On his head were just a few strands of hair, like thin filaments of silver. His hands were knotted and curved like birds' claws, and she couldn't tell what those hands had ever done.

"Yes, yes," he said in a wavering, whispery voice as she slowly came toward him.

Timidly she took the outstretched hand in hers and it felt like ice—like old, cold paper. The shock of her own youthful warmth rang all through Maggie. She felt the years before her with a sort of guilt.

His blinking, watery eyes examined her from a far distance of years and years and years.

"Sit down, please," said the man who had driven her here. He drew up a small chair with carved wooden arms for Maggie and took a straight chair for himself. They were arranged before Mr. St. James who sat shrunken and deep in a large armchair, with a rug over his legs.

Maggie was somehow not surprised when the driver said, "I am Chalcot."

And Mr. St. James motioned with a gnarled hand, "He speaks for me."

"Mr. St. James is not able to speak at length," Mr. Chalcot explained, "so will you please address your speech to me."

Speech! When Maggie was speechless!

"You wished to speak about the tower," he smiled encouragingly, and Maggie saw Mr. St. James lean slightly forward with interest.

"Look around for a moment first," Mr. Chalcot suggested, to put her at ease.

But Maggie's head was stiff as she tried to look and gather her thoughts at the same time. All the beautiful art! She had never seen so much beauty. Paintings and hangings and statues and Oriental chests of teak and ivory. . . . She could have been on another planet, it was so removed from her small world of frame and shingle houses, of linoleum and flowered curtains. . . . She felt like a small brown animal set down in a castle of splendor, and became aware of her heavy brown shoes on the delicate, beautifully patterned rug. She was afraid they would spoil it and tried to sit without letting her feet touch. But it was a terrible strain, so she gently put down just her toes.

And then to her shame—for the rest of her life Maggie would blush when she remembered this—she blurted out in the silent, lovely room, "You must have money to pay the taxes!"

Mr. Chalcot merely smiled when Maggie turned bright red and wanted to cry with embarrassment at the words she couldn't take back. Mr. St. James remained in his bent, patient attitude, waiting.

"Yes, there is money," said Mr. Chalcot.

Having started, Maggie went on, feeling her face flush. "Then why don't you pay the taxes?"

"Is it that you wish to keep the tower?"

"Oh, yes, yes!"

"Why?" he asked simply.

Maggie knew she'd be asked this question, but she still didn't know how to answer it, what to say, or even whom to speak to—Mr. St. James or Mr. Chalcot. She said the first thing she thought of and the words just tumbled out recklessly.

"Because—it holds the moon. I can see it from my window. The moon comes up behind the tower, making it all golden, and then it rises to the top and rests on the peak—"

"Are you afraid the moon will fall if the tower comes down?" asked Mr. Chalcot.

Maggie stared at him. "Oh, no, I'm not that young—" But she looked at him again with a wonder. Everything was so strange. "It—wouldn't, would it?"

Mr. Chalcot laughed, "No. And—?"

"And? Well—it's so beautiful."

"Beautiful? Old, shabby, unfinished, standing in the weeds—beautiful?"

"Oh, yes!" said Maggie.

"Is that all?"

Maggie struggled to find words to fit her thoughts and feelings. She fell back on what the children had said. "It's—different."

"Hm," Mr. St. James murmured.

"And we thought," said Maggie, gaining courage.

"We?" Mr. Chalcot asked abruptly.

"Serena and Tom and Jimmy and I—"

"Children?"

"Yes."

"In the neighborhood?"

"Yes, we all live around the tower."

"Hm," Mr. St. James kept nodding his head.

"What did you think?" Mr. Chalcot prompted.

"We wondered—they wondered—if the tower were finished—"

"Finished! Do you want the tower finished?" Mr. Chalcot eyed her intently.

Maggie had a strange suspicion. Had they just been waiting all this time to be asked to finish the tower? Waiting for an interest in its completion? Then all she would have to say was, "Yes! Please come and finish your building."

And, perversely, Maggie said what she thought was

wrong to say. Passionately, she said the truth. "No!" And thought now she'd done it, she'd ruined everything.

Mr. Chalcot nodded, "Why not?"

"Because it wouldn't be the same—the same difference."

"Hm," Mr. St. James murmured again and smiled at her. It was such a terrible smile, although he meant it to be nice. But he was so old that his gums were shriveled, and he had no teeth. Maggie wondered how it felt to be like that. In his watery eyes was a recognition of her young thoughts, and almost a message to her: One day, yes, you too.

Mr. Chalcot rose suddenly and made Mr. St. James more comfortable in his chair. He lifted him and set him back and plumped the pillows behind his head.

"Interviews are hard for him," he said to Maggie.

But she thought the old man looked better—brighter —than when they'd first walked in. Then Mr. St. James said in his whispery voice, "So there is one, once again— once again." He seemed to draw strength from repeating that.

"Shall I—?" Mr. Chalcot questioned him.

"Yes," Mr. St. James whispered, and nodded at Maggie. "You—full of questions—you will now hear a story."

Mr. Chalcot walked to an ornate desk and brought back a large leather volume which he placed in Maggie's lap. He opened the cover and there, on black paper, was a photograph of a young boy about ten years old, dressed in old-fashioned clothes. He was smiling in the frozen way of most old photographs, and stood stiffly in front of a building that looked familiar to Maggie. . . . With a start she realized it was the town hall!

She gasped, looking at Mr. St. James, certain that it must be he, long, long ago. He smiled at her again with that old and terrible smile, as Mr. Chalcot began to speak. It was meant to be a story without interruption, and Maggie listened with her entire body as the words unfolded.

Mr. Chalcot began by saying, "Once upon a time he was not known as Miguel Sanchez Oliver St. James. . . ."

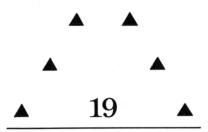

19

ONE OF THE BEST THINGS ABOUT THAT DAY, MAGGIE thought then and ever after, was that neither Mr. St. James nor Mr. Chalcot asked her to keep silent—and yet she knew she must, about most of the things that were said. It was understood that she would have to be selective in what she mentioned to others, as some wise adults were selective.

It was the largest trust she'd ever been given. And to be trusted like that was a gift.

(When Maggie herself became an old lady she saved the same gift for certain people. She would give it to certain grandchildren at special times like Christmas. They would go away to wonder why she had told them a "secret," and then begin to feel as Maggie did that day—responsible, different, with a new grace inside.)

Mr. Chalcot spoke at length in that strange and lovely room that held memories of the latter and greater part of Mr. St. James's life. But Maggie held another part of that life in the book upon her lap. It began when he was not "Miguel Sanchez Oliver St. James," but plain Joseph Henry Stevens, a very ordinary little boy from another part of her own town when it was new, and raw, and closer to its beginnings.

From time to time Maggie would look at the pictures in the book, then at the two men, at the statues, paintings, and tapestries, and at the rug beneath her feet. Sometimes Mr. St. James would smile at her, and at other times he would nod. Part of the nodding was in his always trembling head, but part was really nodding, as if to say, "Yes, yes, that is the way it was. He knows. Yes, yes, that is the way it is."

And, as Maggie listened, the old man deep in the chair became young again. She could see—almost hear—him in his walk through life. . . .

Sometimes he walked, sometimes he ran, sometimes he galloped on horseback. And, yes! Sometimes he rode on trains with steamer trunks and portmanteaus, and looked out windows at the rolling countryside. There were strange trains, in faraway, strange places, and boats rocking across distant seas, and all manners of odd and difficult conveyances. Maggie could feel the heavy tread of elephants and the lurching back and forth on camelback. She could hear the jangling of old streetcars and feel the bounce of tinny, smoking autos. . . .

He had left their small town as a very young man, to

work his way around the world. He was on a search, a quest, for beauty, and began to collect and then sell odd and unusual works of art. In the book were old, yellowing photos of him at that time. In one he stood, young and smiling, dressed in a sailor's uniform, on the deck of a ship. In another he was blackened with coal dust, before a mine.

And there were pictures of other people dressed in foreign costumes, against landscapes of mountains, forests, rivers, deserts, and jungles, and of Mr. St. James, or young Joseph Henry Stevens, standing beside the Pyramids, before the Taj Mahal, on the Great Wall of China. . . .

At one point in his narrative, when he was speaking of a village in a faraway land, Mr. Chalcot stopped to wait for something.

Maggie had just come to a photo of young Mr. Stevens in a wide, woven hat, standing beside a mule train. She looked up in surprise as Mr. Chalcot placed his hand on the book, gently indicating to stop now.

Mr. St. James drew himself up in the low chair, and leaned forward. Trying to speak was costing him something, but he said, "In that ordinary village I saw something. Something—strange," he added, in a voice so suddenly clear it startled Maggie.

He had waited all this time, it seemed, to say these few words. "It was—is—the reason for the tower . . . for everything."

He fell back then, panting, while Mr. Chalcot resumed. "In that village, where people spoke in a different tongue and wore different clothes and worked in different ways, but was in all other respects exactly like your own town," he nodded to Maggie, "Mr. St. James, or Joseph Stevens, as he was then known, observed a peculiar building. . . . It thrust up beside that village, looking singular and quite ugly, as if it had no purpose, no meaning. It disturbed the village symmetry and disturbed and haunted the people—especially the children—"

Maggie interrupted, unable to help it, "It was another tower!"

"No, it was not another tower," Mr. Chalcot smiled at her. "It was—" He glanced at Mr. St. James who nodded. "There is a—representation of it in that book, Miss Sanderson, a little further on."

Maggie, engrossed in the story, was lost between listening and looking, and Mr. Chalcot, leaning over to the book in her lap, carefully turned a few pages.

And she gasped. It was not another old photograph, but a pencil sketch done on paper that had turned brown with age. The drawing was so old and faded that she couldn't see it too clearly, but. . . .

"But it's unfinished, *like* the tower!" breathed Maggie. She could see that much in the blurred outline of the odd structure in the background of the sketch. The foreground was much clearer—children squatting before a village house and staring up at the building that stood in a clearing at the end of a dirt road, with what looked like dense jungle pressing close behind. . . .

And no, it wasn't like the tower—not really. It seemed to be shorter—although tall, not *as* tall—and wider. She strained to look, blinking, trying to see it from the rough sketch. And abruptly Mr. St. James whispered loudly, "Show her!"

Again she looked up from the book in her lap, again surprised when Mr. Chalcot rose and walked to a high, intricately carved cabinet at the far wall of the room.

Maggie watched as he carefully opened the doors, withdrew an object, and brought it back ever so slowly and gingerly on the palms of his hands. Maggie's eyes followed his hands as he placed it, slowly and attentively, on the small table beside Mr. St. James's chair.

Mr. Chalcot then backed away and sat down again, while Maggie stared, wide-eyed, at the same building she had tried to see clearly in the sketch. This had been re-created in clay, and the clay was dark, and hadn't been fired, so there was no smooth glaze, just a rough hardening that made her feel she was looking at the building itself. . . .

And it was so *small*, this reproduction on Mr. St. James's table—below Maggie's eye-level, in fact. And yet she felt that it was enormous, that she was not looking down at it, but looking *up* . . . as those village children must have looked.

She shivered, getting goose-pimples. It was the oddest thing she'd ever seen, even odder than the tower at home. It looked as if it should have been completed in three parts. . . .

On one side was a high-rising turret capped by a small dome. But what should have been its twin, on the opposite side, was incomplete, broke off on a jagged slant, with no dome.

In between was the most mysterious part, and there Maggie's eyes were glued. It was like looking at the unfinished peak.

In between, a long flight of steps made the central part, between the finished and unfinished turrets. But they were also incomplete, unfinished! Wide at the bottom, they tapered, rising up and up—rising *higher* than the one completed turret and dome! That shouldn't have been. Those steps, going up and up were in themselves so strange and disturbing. . . . And they didn't taper to the point one might expect. Instead, they stopped most abruptly—too wide at the top—without something there to complete them—but there was nothing. There was nothing at all up there where there should have been. . . .

She shivered again. It was ugly, just as Mr. Chalcot had said. But it was also beautiful—haunting! Maggie could see the moon rising behind that high flight of steps just as it rose behind the peak on the tower. She could imagine—and almost feel herself as one of those village children—exploring, walking that strange staircase, going up and up, wondering why they rose higher than the turret? Why were the steps there at all, and what did they lead to? What was above and below? What was the mystery behind this odd unfinished building?

As she looked, the small clay figure seemed to grow and loom large in the silent room. It filled the space, and Maggie felt as if the tower were there beside it, too. . . .

For a long time nobody said a word.

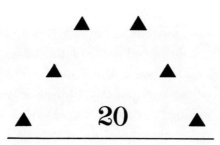

20

Finally Mr. Chalcot spoke again.

"Mr. St. James, or Joseph Stevens, as he was then known, had by that time traveled over a great part of the world, collecting and selling art treasures—"

"Treasures!" came a dim, chuckling sound from the old man in the chair. His whisper blew at Maggie like dry, rustling leaves. "All those years—didn't know—didn't know what real treasure was."

"He was himself so disturbed by that building, Miss Sanderson," Mr. Chalcot smiled at her, "that he forgot all about his business, his collecting and selling of art. Instead he remained for a year in that village, under the shadow of that building, wondering why it affected him and some of the children, as it did. He felt that he couldn't leave until he discovered the secret."

Then Maggie tore her gaze away from the building to stare at him. "The secret?" she whispered, instantly connecting it with the seed of the tower, the reason for building it. And it hadn't been built for any "silly" reason, she was sure.

"There were terrible storms that year," Mr. Chalcot explained, "that destroyed many of the village crops and houses. The children were afraid for the building itself, but it survived, undamaged. Mr. Stevens stayed, helping the people, joining in their work, always haunted and puzzled by that building and the questions it evoked in him.

"He waited for the builder, the architect, whom he had been told would return, hoping to ask him questions. He didn't know how long he would have to wait, nor where else to search for him. But he was prepared to wait years if necessary.

"Finally, after only a year, that man, now an old man, came home to his village to find Joseph Stevens there, eager to question him. His name, by the way, was Miguel—"

"Miguel!" Maggie repeated with surprise. It was now Mr. St. James's first name.

"At first," Mr. Chalcot said softly, "he would not answer any of Mr. Stevens's questions about that odd structure—nor why he had designed it, nor what its purpose could possibly be, nor why it had not been completed. At first he wanted only to know how it affected young Joseph Stevens, what it caused him to feel—"

"You?" Mr. St. James whispered to Maggie. "The tower—?"

"Mr. St. James would like to know how the tower affects you," Mr. Chalcot said for him. "What it causes you to feel."

And again Maggie was helpless, tongue-tied. She couldn't express all those things clearly. All that she managed to murmur was, "It—it makes me wonder—feel wonder."

"Wonder about what?" Mr. Chalcot asked gently.

"Oh—all sorts of things," she said hesitantly. "Just about everything. Things I'd—I'd like to know, to learn about."

"What would you like to learn?" Mr. Chalcot prompted her.

Maggie stared at him. Somehow that was a different question. What would she like to learn! She saw her home, her school, her family and friends—the question filled her inside and out to every inch of her skin. She forgot all about the beautiful room, her shoes on the rug, her timidity. . . .

"Oh, *everything*!" breathed Maggie. "Where I come from, why I'm here, why everything is here—why things even look the way they do! The inside and outside of things. The—the whole universe. Why it's so big and we're so small. And time—if it ever really begins or ends. . . . And, and *me*! Why I'm different from anything else I see—I mean, why I'm not a tree or an animal or—somebody else. Why do I have *different* eyes to look out from? What for? And what's really inside me—everybody? Is it another universe or something else I don't know? . . . And, and where do questions even come from? Why do I have them? What for? And—oh—oh, just *everything!*"

The room rang with silence when she stopped, unable to completely express "everything."

But Mr. St. James nodded, and Mr. Chalcot seemed to understand.

"Yes," he said quietly, "Joseph Stevens had similar questions that he expressed to the man Miguel—"

"Difficult—" Mr. St. James whispered, blinking at Maggie. "Very—difficult."

She felt a shock of understanding. He *knew*. He knew about the "everything" she'd tried to say and couldn't . . . all the unstated questions about the mystery of everything —about even why they were all here right now, together. She suddenly felt very close to him and not embarrassed by her outburst at all.

"They spoke of those questions and of many others as well," Mr. Chalcot continued. "And it was then, in meeting the man Miguel that Mr. Stevens began to understand what he was really searching for. . . . He had thought it was for beauty and collected art, until he found real treasure in a greater search within the questions and the wonder that odd, unfinished building had evoked in him. . . ."

Maggie gazed at the small clay figure, seeing and feeling the tower, too, sensing the connection, wondering how a building could contain such mysteries that everything else became mysterious, too, when you were near it, or looked at it. . . . She shivered, thinking of the wonder the tower made her feel.

"Joseph Stevens found a new search within himself," Mr. Chalcot said. "He questioned everything, and, most of all, the riddle of his own being." He nodded at the clay building and said softly, "That was the secret within it, you see. The questions it caused him to ask."

Then Mr. Chalcot told Maggie that later Miguel had sent Joseph Stevens on to others who could help him in his search. Again he traveled over the world, meeting, in different countries, people who shared his wish for knowledge, and taught him what they knew. There was a man named Sanchez, a Mr. Oliver, and a woman named St. James.

"Although they didn't have answers to everything— nobody does, Miss Sanderson—they were people of some wisdom who had spent years exploring such questions. They helped Mr. Stevens look into his own questions more deeply, and helped him treasure his search.

"When at last Joseph Stevens returned to the land of his birth, and for many reasons did not wish to be known, he took the names of those—you could call them teachers —who had special importance to him. He became Miguel Sanchez Oliver St. James.

"But that building in the small village was the beginning of it all," said Mr. Chalcot. "It was the first of many important ideas he encountered. It caused him to—stop—

and wonder, to ask the questions you have asked. He was deeply affected by it, although it had actually been built for the children. . . .

"What was it?" Mr. Chalcot asked, taking Maggie by surprise.

Her eyes opened wide. She didn't look at the building, and she could see the tower as if it were before them, in the room. Built for the children, by Miguel—the seed of the tower, passed on to Mr. St. James . . . what was it?

The words bubbled out without effort.

"A gift!" said Maggie.

Mr. Chalcot nodded, as did Mr. St. James, smiling.

"But a gift is useless without a receiver," said Mr. Chalcot.

And Mr. St. James raised his old head. "There is one —once again."

Maggie knew he was speaking of her and she was strangely moved. It somehow made her want to cry. But the words lingered and she had to ask, "Once again?"

Mr. Chalcot said, matter-of-factly, "The tower would not have been there otherwise, for all this time. It would have come down long ago. We would not have bothered to pay taxes if there hadn't been another—receiver—once upon a time."

He ended all that he intended to say in the same words with which he'd begun. And the words stayed with Maggie as she rose to leave, handing Mr. Chalcot the book, then taking Mr. James's outstretched hand again. "Once upon a time."

Although it was still cold and dry, it felt different to her. She could feel the warmth of the past in it, all the passion, the life, and the search that had once been Mr. St. James.

Before she had walked into this room, Mr. Chalcot had said, "He is very old." And Maggie knew she was touching the hand of a man so close to death she could almost feel that bridge herself. . . .

He whispered, "Good-bye—young Margaret," as he looked at her with those distant watery eyes that had seen so much, been so far.

The gift of the tower seemed to pass between them.

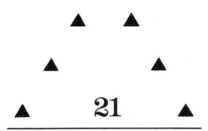

21

WHEN MR. CHALCOT DROVE HER HOME THE CAR NO LONGER seemed strange, or exotic, or in the least "expensive." It was merely another conveyance to get one from here to there. On that afternoon Maggie lost forever any material ideas of high or low, more or less.

Halfway back she began to come into her own skin again, to feel her ordinary, eleven-year-old self. For hours she had not been eleven, nor twelve, nor ten, nor twenty, nor forty, nor eighty. She had been all those years at once, it seemed, but still herself, guessing what she already knew, understanding something beyond her eleven-year-old understanding, something she would know and recognize and greet when she caught up to it again. . . .

Maggie couldn't grasp or hold these swift thoughts and impressions; they were simply there—a kaleidoscope of present feelings and future understanding that were all within her, now and forever.

She had been eleven but not eleven, in some far-off place that was yet so close it included her physical home, the house and garden and picket fence, all the outdoors, and her family and friends. She had been there, and yet very far away, with Mr. St. James.

Around the world, in fact! Maggie smiled, and then saddened, wondering what people would think if they knew his real name, who he really had been? If they knew everything, they would think he was crazy. "The crazy man!" It would be proved. Who else would travel around the world on a quest for beauty, and then on a personal search, seeking answers to big questions, even to the riddle of himself—unless he were "crazy"? Who else would build an unfinished tower?

She looked out at the countryside, at the long afternoon shadows falling across pastures and hills, making the landscape both brighter and darker. She thought about gifts.

The sun was a gift, and so was the restfulness of darkness. But they were big gifts, from God or the universe, to everybody and every growing thing. She had been given a personal gift this afternoon—that of being trusted. And that was a big, a real gift. What other real gifts like that could there be, Maggie wondered?

Sometimes, she supposed, a gift could be an example. It might be written in the face or actions of a person. Her mother's courage when she was ill, her teacher's patience when Maggie didn't finish everything . . . yes, they were big and real gifts. They were enduring. Maggie would never forget!

And the tower? Something was written there, too, and in that other strange building. The gift of evoking questions, of causing feelings of wonder. How could all that be designed in stone? "That was the secret within it," Mr. Chalcot had said. . . .

But how could that be? Maggie felt there was still a secret—a secret behind the secret. She was missing something, she thought. Something still eluded her. . . .

Mr. Chalcot could not have been more properly the "chauffeur" on the way back, nor more sensitive to Maggie's quiet reflections. He didn't speak at all, and she remembered to draw the curtains as they approached the town. He drew up so gently in front of the Hotel Imperial that she was hardly aware they had stopped.

Maggie didn't get out immediately; she stayed in the back for a moment, filled with questions, so many questions that she'd never be able to ask. She didn't ask Mr. Chalcot what deep connection he had with Mr. St. James, or if he were, himself, one of those important people in Mr. St. James's life. She felt he was. Later, Maggie would even wonder if Chalcot was his real name. . . .

But there was one question she had to ask.

"The other—" said Maggie. "The other one who—who noticed the tower. Was it a child?"

"Oh, yes," Mr. Chalcot turned to smile at her. "Indeed it was."

"Long ago?"

"Quite long ago."

"And—how did you know about it? How did you find out?"

"From time to time we have come to look at the tower. One day, long, long ago, we came to find that people were complaining. A child—a little boy—had gone up one night and painted the peak all gold."

When she got home, Maggie hung up her brown jumper carefully, fingering the skirt of the material, wishing she could keep it always, for it had taken her someplace so special. She hung up her white blouse in the same way, feeling that she was leaving part of her experience with the clothes, as she shut the closet door.

She put on an old blouse and skirt and moved, head down, to her bed by the window. She was a little hesitant, even a bit afraid, to look out at the tower now. Would it be the same to her now, after this afternoon, still mysterious but still her friend? Would it look as special and beautiful, now that she knew more? Or would it be somehow different? Would it be less—or more?

Very slowly she raised her eyes—and caught her breath.

It *was* different! It was *more*, more beautiful, more mysterious, more of a secret than ever! The sunset had outlined it in pink and red and gold, and even the charred peak had a rosy hue. But it wasn't the color that moved her. She seemed to see the old face of Mr. St. James before the tower, and knew she would never really see him again —and yet he would somehow be with her, always. He could never be "finished" or "ended." *Nothing* could be!

The tower spoke it, saying nothing was ever really finished or ended—there was always more life, more questions, more wonder.

Maggie saw the little boy going up the tower steps so long ago to paint the peak with gold—and suddenly the whole world seemed to explode within her! She was not *alone* with her longings and feelings! Even if she couldn't tell the other children everything—*he* had felt the same. That little boy, grown old now, maybe dead, but never ended, never finished—he was with her, too.

He had felt the same, that the tower was not an accident, that it came from somewhere deep and true, that it represented something real—and its roots reached out far in space and time.

The gift!

It was from Miguel Sanchez Oliver St. James—yes, from all of them—and from Joseph Henry Stevens, who had built the tower and left it unfinished *deliberately*. Somehow she had always known that, from some deep-down place inside.

And how could that gift of wonder—and hope—be designed in stone? How could a building contain all that?

As Maggie looked, the secret behind the secret seemed to speak from every stone. Like the odd structure with the haunting flight of steps in that faraway village that the man Miguel had designed, the tower was more than a rising of gray stone and empty windows and a deliberately unfinished peak that held the moon . . . although it was all that, too.

But it was the *love* behind the gift that mattered—that was what the tower contained! Love was the secret behind the secret, was what had called her, through the tower, all her young years. Love. The loving wish for others. . . .

And somehow, Maggie thought, she had always known that, too—from some deep-down place in her soul.

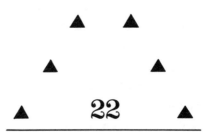

22

THE HEAT OF SUMMER AGAIN ENCLOSED THE TOWN. IT wrapped around everything like a great hot blanket, trapping everyone in its numerous folds. The sun seemed careless of small people below who could find no relief, who sought escape in small words that ran at the bottom of things. A new sort of gossip made its way through town.

"Crazy man's paid his taxes!"

"Tower's not going to come down!"

"Somebody's going to miss out on a nice property."

"Crazy place! Not fit for anything."

"But the platform at the top's going back up—"

"I wonder why?"

When Serena and Tom and Jimmy heard all this, they were agog with curiosity and hung around Maggie's front yard, on the sidewalk next to her fence, waiting to question her. But they left, realizing something was wrong, when they saw the doctor come.

Maggie's mother was suffering terribly again, in the

unusual heat wave. The doctor said, "She does have a heart condition, yes. But it's manageable. If she's careful, she still has a long and useful life before her."

He scared Maggie silly, and for a few weeks all she could think of was her mother. She did all the things she'd done before, while outside on the tower, men came to build another floor at the top. They scraped off the charred gold paint and left the peak as gray and clean as it was born.

Mr. Meyers came to look at the lot again—making a loud event of it—and went away muttering and complaining and still threatening to do something about it.

One day, when it was a breath cooler, and her mother was a little better, Maggie saw the children outside. She ran out for a moment, and they pummeled her with questions.

"Was it *you*, Maggie?" Serena asked. "Did you get an answer to your letter?"

"Did you see him?" asked Tom. "And where? Where was he?"

"What was he like?" Jimmy demanded, and they all spoke on top of each other. . . .

"Is he really crazy?"

"What did he say?"

"Did he tell you why he built the tower?"

"Did you tell him about us, that we wanted to keep it?"

"What did *you* say?"

"What happened, Maggie?"

It was too much! She hadn't been able to think what to tell them—how much—but she felt a responsibility to them. What could she tell them in a way they'd understand? She hadn't even told her mother that she'd been to the city!

Maggie knew her hurried answers weren't very satisfactory. She saw bewildered looks in their eyes as she replied vaguely that yes, she'd seen him—but please don't tell anybody else! No, he wasn't crazy. They'd talked about a lot of things. Yes, she had mentioned all of them. . . .

She absolutely couldn't tell them *why* he had built the tower. That needed some thinking about. And every minute she was outside, she felt she should be inside, with her mother. . . .

Then, Serena, with a very nice smile, said something that really touched Maggie. "You can tell us later—but thank you for going to see him, Maggie. Thank you for the tower."

And the boys echoed gruffly, "Yeah, thanks, Mag— and—hope your mother gets better."

They went off, respecting her duties, even somehow respecting her hesitation about answering questions about the tower. They must have caught a glimmer of something.

Maggie went inside, blinking hard, wondering even more how and what she could tell them. They deserved to

know *something*! It made her feel very quiet and subdued, and even guiltier about having lied to her mother
about where she'd been that day. . . .

She had never lied quite like that before! If she didn't
correct it, Maggie thought, it would plague her for the
rest of her life. But she couldn't say anything now; her
mother wasn't well enough.

On another day, when she was washing dishes at the
sink, Maggie saw Jerry Forbes standing on the sidewalk,
looking at the tower. Her mother was sleeping, so again
she ran out for just a moment, this time to see him.

He saw at once that she had serious things and a
worry on her mind, so he just asked simply, "What happened, Maggie? It isn't going to be sold or torn down."

"I know—"

"You wrote, and got an answer—and saw him!" Jerry
said, guessing correctly. "So he isn't dead."

"Wasn't—then," whispered Maggie. "If I told you—
anything—would you write about it for the paper?"

Jerry Forbes looked, not at Maggie, but at the tower
for some time. Finally he said, "*He* never wrote about it or
explained it, did he? So why should I? It's a mystery. And
maybe you know something about it," he smiled at her,
"but, Maggie, I don't know enough. And I don't think I'd
write about it even if I did."

He looked again at the tower. "Let it be."

Maggie loved him for that seriousness and for not
questioning her, and for seeing that it was a mystery.

"Come back to see me when you can," he sang out over his shoulder as he walked away.

Jerry Forbes brightened Maggie's day. There *were* people who could be serious about important things and light and happy at the same time! Life could—or maybe should—be joyous, even in the middle of the biggest mysteries.

Another secret, she thought, feeling a singing deep inside when she went back in. Joy of life! Another gift—this time from Jerry Forbes. It helped her settle her doubts about finally confessing to her mother that she'd lied. She couldn't do it right now—that would be selfish—just to reorder and settle things within herself. But when the right time came—Maggie paused in the hallway, looking at her mother asleep in the parlor—oh, yes! She could tell her where she'd really been, gladly, and accept any consequences—because she'd *had* to go . . . and she could say that, freely.

That night the spell of heat finally broke. The world came apart in a tremendous, crashing storm that felled trees, broke power lines, and flooded the streets of the town. The next day everyone looked at the tower and at the single peak that still remained, piercing the sky. . . .

"Darn thing's never going to come down."

"Eerie, the way it stays up there—"

Cool breezes followed the storm, running through the streets, blowing in open windows. Maggie's mother abruptly felt much better. Finally she could relax—and

Maggie also relaxed, although every time she looked at her mother she could see the old face of Mr. St. James. And her own face, in years to come. . . .

She was plagued with love, an intense, deep love that included joy of life, that wanted to reach out and embrace everything and bring it in close, to protect and keep forever, and ever—everything. She knew that was why she hadn't always finished everything—she loved too much, to put an end to anything. Only the tower helped her, reminding her that there was no end to anything, and that love went on and on. . . .

There came a night when the moon was going to rise full again. And because she had said so little to Serena and Tom and Jimmy, Maggie invited them to her house, to her room, where they could all look out the window together.

They all sat on her bed to watch the full, round moon rise. It had a yellow glint this night; it was almost pure gold. It rose behind the tower, then drifted above to rest —a shimmering ball balancing atop the peak.

"It's a gift for us," said Maggie about the tower, "to help us wonder, to help us look—to remind us of things."

"Unfinished things," said Serena.

"Like us?" wondered Tom.

"Maybe nothing is ever finished," said Jimmy. "Maybe everything goes on and on."

They looked in silence for a time and then Serena said, "It was nice of him to give it to us."

The moon floated up and away, but light remained on the peak beneath. One day soon, Maggie knew, she would go up to paint it gold again, as the little boy had done so long ago. . . .

She thought of Mr. St. James and all his friends and guides, of all the gifts of wonder that had passed between them, and of the mystery of life, without beginning or end. . . .

"You know," said Tom, "it—well, it sort of *bothers* you—"

"It's supposed to," whispered Maggie. "That's what it's for."

The tower remained, thrusting high from the weedy lot where no trees grew, disturbing and haunting the townspeople, especially the children.

"Built by a crazy man," people continued to say.

"Must have been crazy to build such a thing!"

"When that peak falls—"

But it didn't. It remained, remarkably, for years and years, while new generations of children grew, and some of them looked—and wondered.

When Maggie and her friends grew up and spread over the skin of the earth in their various directions, they never forgot the gift of the unfinished tower, especially Maggie, who made it her business later in life, to keep the tower there, one of her many gifts to many children.

When she left that small town on a search of her

own, she carried with her always a vision of the mysterious peak beneath the moon. And a sense of wonder and
purpose and love stayed with her always, her whole, long
life.